KILLERS DON'T RETIRE

Mellor heard what he had been waiting for—his name whispered by one of the men a dozen feet away at the end of the rough-sawed bar. Not even in this place could he remain anonymous. His breath sighed out softly and something new came over him, like wariness in an animal that expects to be attacked.

But perhaps it would be different here. Perhaps, even though he was recognized, he would be allowed to finish his drink and leave. He reached for his glass, picked it up, carried it halfway to his mouth—

"Hey, mister!"

Mellor's hand stopped, the glass still several inches away from his mouth. Resigned, he put it down. He knew, then, that he wouldn't finish it until he had killed another man . . .

Charter Westerns by Lewis B. Patten

The Ruthless Range

Lewis B. Patten

CHARTER BOOKS, NEW YORK

THE RUTHLESS RANGE

A Charter Book / published by arrangement with
the author

PRINTING HISTORY
Berkley edition / March 1978
Charter edition / January 1984
Second printing / August 1986

ISBN: 0-441-74181-9

Charter Books are published by The Berkley Publishing Group,
200 Madison Avenue, New York, New York 10016.
PRINTED IN THE UNITED STATES OF AMERICA

Chapter 1

Rain slanted almost horizontally out of the northeast, driven by a wind that bent the tall, straight lodgepole pines and made a sustained roar whistling through them. Overhead, black clouds scudded along, sometimes obscuring the tops of the low hills through which the solitary horseman rode.

He wore a tattered slicker that flapped noisily in the wind. Water cascaded from his hatbrim in front. His horse slipped and slid dangerously on the slick, wet clay underfoot.

Jason Mellor rode hunched against the wind and cold, his face dark and still, his eyes bright between lids narrowed against the driving rain. His mouth was a gash in his dripping face, straight and thin and hard.

His left hand held the reins, his right hung loosely at his side, thumb touching the saddle skirt. He seemed a part of this harsh and bitter land, as harsh and bitter as the land itself. But there was patience apparent in him

1

too—patience with the discomfort heaped upon him by the elements: patience with the slowness of the miles ahead.

Gradually the fury of the storm abated. It settled down to a steady drizzling, without much wind. Man and horse plodded along, down out of the hills and the lodgepole pines, into sagebrush and grass and rolling plain. At last, near dusk, Jason spotted the settlement ahead.

It wasn't much, but then he never expected much any more. It consisted of a single street formed by a two-track road that wandered in off the prairie and, after a hundred yards, wandered out again. Buildings on both sides of the street numbered six in all.

There was a livery barn separated from a two-story hotel by a vacant lot. Next to the hotel was the saloon, and next to that the mercantile store. Across the street there was a one-room log building, sod-roofed and probably the original building there. Beside it was a house built of rough-sawed, unpainted boards.

Sight of the settlement did not increase his pace, although his mind was pondering the comfort of a bed in the hotel tonight, a meal cooked by someone other than himself, and a drink or two at the bar of the saloon. And somehow his thoughts took a measure of the bitterness from his face.

He plodded in along the muddy road, halted at the saloon and swung stiffly to the ground. He looped his horse's reins around the rail and waded through the mud to the boardwalk, where he stopped long enough to stamp part of the mud from his boots. Going on, he removed his hat and batted it against his leg. A shower of rain water sprayed from it; then he put it on again.

The saloon was no more impressive than the town itself. It held half a dozen homemade tables with benches on both sides of them. The bar was rough-sawed two-inch planks. The backbar was made of the same material, and held a quantity of glasses, a bucket of water to wash them in, and half a dozen gallon stoneware jugs, unlabeled, holding, no doubt, the whisky, which was probably distilled within a hundred miles of here.

But after the rain, and cold, and mud, it all looked good to Jason, perhaps because there were other people here.

A bartender. A drunk with his head down on his arm at the end of one of the tables. Three men playing stud at another table. And three at the bar.

He took his slicker off, hung it on a nail beside the door and crossed the sawdust floor to the bar. He flexed his chilled and stiffened hands as he said, "One of those jugs and a glass."

He tried not to look at the other three lined up at the bar, but he knew they were looking at him. His face settled and hardened almost imperceptibly.

When he heard them whispering, he stiffened, turned his head and put his steady glance on them. They looked away and he uncorked the jug and poured his glass half full.

He gulped the whisky, made a face at the rawness of it, then poured his glass half full a second time. He seemed to be waiting, listening, the set of his head intent.

He heard what he had been waiting for. His name, whispered by one of the men a dozen feet away at the end of the rough-sawed bar.

"Mellor! Hell yes, it is!"

Not even in this place, then, could he remain anonymous. His breath sighed out softly and the quality of waiting left him. Yet now something new came over him, like wariness in an animal that expects to be attacked.

There was a pattern in these things, he thought, that never varied. It was as though it were all some sort of macabre play, with everyone rehearsed and familiar with his lines. In a dozen towns, in a dozen parts of the sparsely settled land, it had happened to him before.

But perhaps it would be different here. Perhaps, even though he was recognized, he would be allowed to finish his drink and leave. Perhaps he could still spend the night in that bed at the hotel. Perhaps he could still have a meal cooked by someone other than himself.

He reached for his glass, picked it up, carried it halfway to his mouth.

"Hey, mister!"

His hand stopped, the glass still several inches away from his mouth. Resignedly he put it down. He wouldn't finish it now until he had killed a man.

He glanced in the direction of the voice. "What?"

One of the three pushed himself away from the bar and turned to face Jason. He said, "Ain't your name Mellor? Jason Mellor?"

"That's right."

"The gunfighter?"

Jason shrugged without reply.

"You don't look like so much. Bet you made that big name you got shootin' down drunks an' men that didn't know one end of their damn guns from the other."

Jason shrugged again. "Maybe." He stared at the man facing him without much interest.

The man was young, under twenty-five. They almost always were. Present in the young man's face was nervous fear, because he was facing more than a man— he was facing a legend. But present as well was a recklessness that announced his determination to prove that legends were for kids and cowards but not for him.

Excitement was present too. Because here was the biggest gamble in the world—a hand of showdown in which he would bet his life against Jason Mellor's fame. In a single second he would either die or become known as the man who had beaten Jason Mellor to the draw.

A lousy cause to die for, thought Jason sourly. Yet many had died for it and many more would. He said, still patiently, "You don't think you can die, but you can. Let me buy you a drink. There's nothing for you and me to quarrel about. I don't even know your name."

"It's Nordyke. Burt Nordyke. It's a name a lot of people will be knowin' from today on."

Jason said, "Have a drink and go home, Burt." He was tired and cold and wet, and for some reason the whiskey had left a nauseous knot in his stomach instead of a pleasant warmth. He didn't want Burt Nordyke's face to parade through his dreams tonight. He didn't want to toss all night in a clammy sweat as he lived the gunfight over and over in his dreams.

Nordyke said shrilly, "No, by God! I wanta see if you're as good as they say you are."

"Let's set up a target, then."

Nordyke stared at him, confusedly. "Are you scared of me? Or are you just plain yellow all the way through?"

Jason said softly. "Let it drop, Burt. I'll still buy you that drink."

"I'm particular who I drink with."

"But not who you fight with. That it?"

Jason tried to stifle the irritation that was rising in him. He didn't want this quarrel. He was tired and wet and beginning to feel sick. He only wanted to be let alone. But weariness was having its effect. He tried again to kill his stirring irritability and failed.

"Man don't ask for pedigrees before he kills a snake."

"And I'm a snake?" Jason could feel the acceleration of his heart. He could feel the blood pounding faster through his veins. He felt warmer and steadier, and he was as ready now as he would ever be.

He didn't know how long the insults would go on, but he did know he would endure them no matter how long they lasted. Only when Burt Nordyke's hand streaked for his gun would he himself move.

"You are. A slimy, crawling snake."

"It won't work, Burt. I won't draw first against you. You can still turn and walk out of here. You can still take that drink I offered you. Or you can pull your gun. But don't take forever making up your mind. It's suppertime."

The blood drained out of Burt's face and this, too, was a familiar sign. Presently his mouth would firm, his eyes would narrow. Then he'd make an almost frantic grab for his gun.

Why, Jason wondered, didn't he just leave his gun in its holster? Why didn't he let Burt shoot?

His mouth twisted wryly. He had wondered the same thing often enough before, and a couple of times he had tried. Yet somehow, when his opponent's hand began to move, thinking stopped and reflex seemed to take over his actions. His own hand moved and his own gun came out of its holster and up. . . .

Burt's mouth firmed out. An eyelid twitched. Jason said softly, "You don't have to do it, Burt. Turn away and let it pass."

"No!" The moment had come at last. Burt's eyelids narrowed and his hand began to move as he made an almost frantic grab for his gun.

Jason's own hand was moving instantly, driven by reflexes he could not control. He felt the worn, smooth, cold grip of the .44 against his palm, felt its weight as he hefted it. He felt the hammer against his thumb and heard it click.

But these actions were automatic, and with his eyes and thoughts he was watching Burt. The man was fast. His hand was blurred with the swiftness of motion. The slap of it against the grip of the gun was audible, as was the click of the hammer coming back. But Jason's gun was already up, almost in line.

His finger tightened reflexively on the trigger. Yet before it had tightened enough, before the gun fired, he managed to halt all movement in himself, something he had never managed before.

Perhaps Burt could stop. Perhaps, seeing Jason's gun lined squarely on him and ready, he could stop the motion of his own right hand, and live.

Apparently Burt could not stop. His gun came up and lined itself on Jason.

Jason could wait no longer. For a second time his finger tightened on the triggeer of his gun.

The buck of it against his palm was a familiar yet strangely ugly thing, as was the acrid bite of powdersmoke in his nose. Burt's gun roared close behind, its sound like an echo of Jason's own.

Burt grunted heavily as the slug took him in the chest. He flinched and took an involuntary backward step. The expression his face held was one of surprise, and shock. He had been so sure. . . .

Untouched, Jason switched his glance from Burt to the others standing at the bar. He said, "Steady, all of you. Don't move."

Burt sat down. He bent over forward as though he were sick. His arms clasped his belly as if it hurt, yet Jason knew the wound was higher up. Then slowly he fell sideways and lay there curled up like a boy asleep.

A feeling crept over Jason, of sour regret because something had just been done that could never be repaired.

Anger came to him too, towering anger because he had again been forced into something against his will, because his destiny had been snatched ruthlessly out of his hands.

Over at the poker table the three sat frozen, staring dumbly at Jason, who said harshly and angrily, "I tried to talk him out of it. You knew him. Why the hell didn't you help?"

The three at the poker table got up silently and went outside. The drunk lifted his head from the table and stared stupidly at the body on the sawdust floor. One of the two who had been with Burt said, "We ain't going to try anything. Can we get him out of here?"

Jason said, "Go ahead."

With his gun still in his hand he watched while they knelt and lifted Burt Nordyke up. Staggering, they carried him out the door.

Jason holstered his gun. He turned back toward the bar and stared with distaste at his drink. Suddenly he lifted it and gulped it down.

The bartender watched him steadily, only averting his glance when Jason looked at him. He muttered, "I'd make tracks, mister, if I was you. I saw the way you held off, but that won't help you none. Burt's got a brother and his brother's got friends. There'll be ten men after you soon's they know that Burt is dead."

Jason stared at the jug in front of him. The dead men always had friends or relatives. Sometimes they trailed him and sometimes they did not. But a man got to wondering when one of the relatives or friends of the one he had killed would shoot him in the back.

He shrugged, and his breath came out in a weary sigh. "All right. Thanks for warning me."

He tossed a quarter on the bar, turned away, walked to the door and took his slicker down. Shrugging into it, he went out into the drizzling rain. There were provisions behind his saddle for a meal tonight. Tomorrow maybe he could shoot some meat.

The bed at the hotel was out of the question, and so was the meal cooked by somebody else. If he went right now perhaps the rain would hide his trail.

He untied his horse, swung astride, turned the animal's head and rode west into the gathering night.

Chapter 2

The drizzle stopped before he had gone a mile and when it did he cursed mildly to himself. But there was no help for it, and no longer any point in killing his horse trying to put distance between himself and the town he had just left. He was making deeply indented tracks that a fool could follow. If he stopped now and slept, both he and his horse would be fresh tomorrow. The ground would have firmed by then and the going would be both faster and easier. Besides, on firm ground his trail could not be so easily followed.

His patience was wearing thin. Too often he fled a town like this, because a quarrel had been forced on him. He touched absently the stock of the rifle protruding from the saddle boot. One of these days he would not run. He'd stop, and turn them back whimpering and licking their wounds, carrying their dead.

He covered about ten miles before he stopped. The

sky was clearing now, and stars winked in its velvet expanse. He picketed his horse beneath a tree where the ground was less soggy than elsewhere. He ate his rations cold because he did not dare risk a fire. Then he rolled himself in his soggy blankets.

He shivered miserably for a long, long time, but at last he went to sleep.

It was Burt Nordyke's face that paraded through his dreams. He was traveling along a road walled on either side like a corridor, so that turning off was impossible. Ahead of him disembodied faces hung in the air, blocking his passage. All the faces were Burt Nordyke's.

Reaching one, he would fire and the face would disappear. But there was always another one ahead. And whenever he looked behind he saw a mob pursuing him. Each face in the mob bore a marked resemblance to Nordyke's, and yet was different.

He awoke half an hour before dawn and got hastily to his feet. His blankets were muddy and wet, but he'd get no chance to dry them today. He rolled them in his slicker, then saddled and bridled his horse and mounted. He rode out again, east, and as light began to grow grayly in the sky he started looking for ways to hide his trail.

The plain stretched ahead of him for what seemed like a thousand miles, rolling fresh after the rain of the day before. Rocky escarpments and table-topped mesas raised themselves in the distance. Occasionally the plain was gashed by a canyon thickly grown with cedars and jackpine.

He tried to find rocky ground, and canyons with their carpets of needles to cushion his horse's tracks. The sun came up in the east and its heat rapidly dried the ground.

Now, in broad daylight, Jason kept his horse below the horizon all the time so that he would not be skylined for the men behind. But in midmorning, halted in rocks at the bluff, he stared behind and saw them coming, like ants crawling relentlessly across the plain.

They were so far away that he couldn't count them for sure—but ten would not miss their number by much. Again he cursed mildly to himself. He was tired and so was his horse. But there would be no rest today.

The gun at his side and the reputation he had made without ever wanting to—suddenly he hated both, for they had cost him everything he valued in life. His wife, Edie, who had stayed with him for nearly two years but who had finally run away, tired of the moving from town to town, tired of hardship and hunger and Jason's promises that he meant and tried to keep but never could. They had cost him the friendship of other men; roots, sons.

There had to be an escape, he thought. There had to be a way. But he had tried the ways he knew—changing his appearance, going far from the places where he was known. Neither had worked. Someone who knew his face always drifted in. Someone always saw behind the beard.

He stared down at his weary horse, at his worn boots and scuffed saddle. He thought of the single twenty-dollar gold piece in the pocket of his pants. A lifetime, almost and all he had to show for it was this.

It had started so innocently, so damned easily. It began with a growing boy whose head was full of dreams, who loved guns and couldn't get enough of shooting them. It began because a boy with a gun trying to act like a man is ridiculous, and because a boy's pride is an overly touchy thing. It ended with a challenge and a man dead in the street of the town where Jason Mellor had lived then.

There was always something familiar in the Burt Nordykes who challenged him. In each of them he saw himself fifteen years ago. The only difference was that the Burt Nordykes died and Jason Mellor had lived to become the best.

The pursuers gained on him a little that day, but he nullified the gain by traveling late into the night. He slept, and dreamed the same dream again, and awoke to a day exactly like the last. This day they gained again, but this night he could not go on, and neither could his horse. He stopped when his pursuers did, and started with less of a lead on the following day.

A bleak certainty was growing in him, one he had never felt before. They'd catch him this time and, if he weren't dead when they got their hands on him, they'd string him up. They'd leave him dangling to rot in the sun and rain and sleet and wind.

He urged his horse to a faster pace, though he knew the animal could not maintain it long. And he began to look for a place to make a stand.

He found it eventually, in midafternoon, at the top of a rocky escarpment higher than most of those he had passed in the last three days. His horse scrambled, trembling, up the shaly slope and stopped, heaving and wheezing, at its top.

Jason swung down, swiftly unsaddled and dropped the reins. The horse stood listlessly, not even bothering to eat. He wouldn't go much farther.

Jason returned through the rocks to a spot from which he could see the plain for thirty miles. The pursuers were closer than they had been, no more than a couple of miles away. Watching them with no great show of interest, he counted nine of them.

He squatted comfortably with his rifle in the shade of a towering, jagged rock and watched a sand lizard climb upon a nearby rock and stare at him with unwinking, beady eyes. He fished absently in his soggy shirt pocket for his thin sack of tobacco. He rolled a smoke and lit it, wryly observing that there was only enough tobacco for a couple more—one when the fight was the hottest, near dusk tonight; and one just before he died.

Morbid thoughts, but they came against his will and stayed. He wondered how Edie was, and where she was, and if she had married again. Quite possibly she had, he thought. He found himself hoping so and visualizing her in the surroundings she deserved, a respectable home in a civilized town with a man who loved her and could take care of her.

Looking down, he saw that the nine were only a mile away. He checked the loads in his gun, eased the hammer back to half cocked and waited patiently. Let them come to within three hundred yards. Let them come on unsuspectingly to the bottom of the slope. Then knock their horses down as fast as the gun would shoot. If he were successful in putting them afoot perhaps he still might have a chance.

The sun sank relentlessly down the western sky, and as relentlessly the nine came on. To half a mile. To a quarter mile. And Jason Mellor raised his gun.

He rested it carefully against the rock and, as they

urged their horses up the shaly slope, he drew a bead on a horse's chest and fired.

He heard the bullet strike and saw the horse rear and fall backward down the slope. But already he had a bead on the second one. Never mind the men, he thought. Get the horses. As many as you can.

The second horse shied sideways, lost his footing and rolled. Jason heard a screech of pain from the man as the horse rolled over him. He drew a third bead and fired once more. This time the horse whirled and bolted, three-legged, diagonally down the slope.

All was confusion down there. Men yelled frantically. Then they reined aside and sank spurs into their horses' sides. In a group they thundered along parallel to the slope toward the shelter of a gulch a quarter mile away.

With his rifle, Jason followed them, and fired at the leading horse. It too went down, throwing its rider clear. He fired again and missed. Then he got no chance to fire again, for they reached the gulch and disappeared into it.

Below, two of the men he had put afoot were dragging the third toward the gulch. Jason had a clear shot at them, but refused it. They reached the gulch and also disappeared.

Four horses, he thought. Four out of nine. He should have done better than that, and would have, except for the presence of the gulch.

Shrugging fatalistically, he got slowly to his feet. Trying to stay covered, he made his way upslope toward his horse. Tomorrow was another day. Tomorrow he could lay a similar ambuscade and perhaps turn them back once and for all.

He felt the blow of the bullet a split second before he heard the report. It drove him forward, numb, like the blow of a sledgehammer from behind.

One instant he was on his feet; the next he was prone, his face grinding into the rocks and dirt. A flood of warm blood drenched his back and side. His brain reeled. He tried to move and failed.

Now more reports burst from the valley floor. Bullets ricocheted from rocks nearby and whined away into distance. Burst of dirt showered him.

Feeling returned, bringing with it both pain and the power to move. He rolled, and slid downward until he banged up against the base of the rock he had left only seconds before. He stared at the blueness of the sky, at the sinking sun, at the puffy white clouds drifting so lazily up there. This, then, was to be the place where he would die. This was the end of the road.

Slowly his anger began to grow. Die here he might, but his dying would not be an easy thing for those who had caused it. Even at the last minute, when Burt Nordyke's gun was in his hand, Jason had held off firing his own. He had tried to save Nordyke's life, but he hadn't been permitted to. He wasn't going to be shot down like a marauding coyote for no more than that.

He rolled, and came to his hands and knees, wondering how bad a wound he had. His rifle lay five feet away, upslope from him.

He crawled toward it. Again the rifles shouted on the valley floor, and again dust spurts kicked up around his crawling form. But he reached the rifle, dragged it to him, and slid back to the shelter of the rock.

They knew he was hit and they only had to wait. No

targets showed themselves down there and nothing appeared on which he could line his sights.

The sun settled toward the hills in far distance on the western horizon. With agonizing slowness. In darkness, he knew, was his only chance. It wasn't much of a chance, at that, and at best could scarcely last longer than dawn.

How bad a wound? Rolling onto his side, he pulled at his soggy shirt and got the shirttail out. His underwear was drenched and scarlet. He unbuttoned it and peeled it back from the wound.

Bad enough, he thought. The bullet had torn through his rib cage in the rear, probably chipping a rib as it did so. It had come out in front, having passed through close underneath the chipped or broken rib.

Exertion and pain had turned him pale, had brought out a cold bath of sweat all over his body. He settled back and rested and, when he felt up to it, rebuttoned his underwear and shirt. The wound, in itself, was not too serious, he guessed. If he had a bed and care for a few days. . . .

But he hadn't. He did not even have a piece of cloth with which to make a compress for the wound—unless he used a piece from one of his blankets, and they were up in the rocks where his saddle lay.

Bleeding, then, loss of blood was the greatest danger to him right now. To make the bleeding stop, he must remain as still as he could.

He settled himself, therefore, in a position from which he could see the gulch and fire at anyone leaving it, without moving himself. He waited, while waves of weakness rolled through his mind and made it reel. The rim of the sun dipped below the western horizon and the clouds flamed orange and gold.

A horse thundered suddenly out of the gulch, whirled and headed away from Jason toward the far end of the butte. He lowered his head to the sights of his gun, took careful aim, pulled ahead slightly to lead the racing horseman, and fired.

The horse went down in a spectacular crash, somersaulting end over end several times. After that it lay kicking and trying to get up.

The man lay still, stunned, for several long minutes while the sun sank out of sight in the west. Then he got to his hands and knees and stared around dazedly for several moments before he looked up at the spot where Jason was.

Apparently realizing at last what had happened, he got up and sprinted, limping, back toward the ravine. Jason let him go. He had bought his time. They would wait until it was dark, until they could safely leave the shelter of the gulch. And Jason would get away.

Provided, of course, that he could catch his horse. Provided he could throw the saddle on without passing out from pain and the exertion.

Get away. It was a bitter, sour phrase with no more than temporary meaning. Because when the sun came up tomorrow they'd be on him again, and they couldn't fail next time. He was too badly hurt. He couldn't travel fast, and there would be times when he wouldn't be able to stay awake. They'd get him and hang him, wounded, from the nearest tree.

He had often wondered what the moment of dying would be like. He had known it was coming and he hadn't expected it to be easy for him. But to hang . . .

He stared bleakly at the gulch below, watching as gray crept across the plain, deepening, darkening. . . . When he could no longer see the gulch itself he got painfully to his feet and staggered up the slope toward the place where he had left his horse. His jaw was clenched hard against the weakness and the pain.

Chapter 3

There were times when he thought he could not go on. It seemed to take him an hour to catch his horse and lead it back. He made half a dozen tries before he got the saddle on, and then he had to rest nearly five minutes before he could summon the strength to cinch it down.

Mounting was an ordeal of equal intensity. Several times the horse almost bolted away from him, frightened both by the smell of blood and the strange actions of the man he knew so well. But at last Jason got himself into the saddle and reined away from the spot.

He drowsed as he rode, in spite of his efforts to stay awake. He doubted if they'd try pursuing him tonight, for they must know how easy it would be when daylight came. But he knew they might. And he was afraid that if he let go . . . if he let himself go to sleep . . . he would fall out of the saddle and never get into it again.

Pain came in waves and with each wave his weakness was greater than it had been before. He lost track of time, he seemed to have been plodding along like this for days.

He stared almost disinterestedly at the flickering fire ahead. Realization that it was not a hallucination took several minutes to penetrate his consciousness.

Not that it mattered. Whoever had made that fire would neither shelter nor hide him. But they might dress his wound. They might possibly give him some food. They might help him on his horse afterward, having given him increased strength to go on.

He turned the slight amount necessary to head straight toward the fire. A few moments later he pulled up beside it, without the strength to speak or to dismount.

There must have been a dozen men in the vicinity of the fire. They gathered to stare up at him. One was tall, taller than Jason himself. And gaunt. And dark from sun and wind and dust.

This one said. "Get him down. Get him down and we'll take a look at him."

"Si, señor."

Hands reached up and he fell out of his saddle into them. Pain was like a knife in his back and blackness swam across his vision, blotting out the light of the fire and the faces it illuminated.

There was a dream that persisted in his mind, a dream that had all the substance of reality and yet could not have been more than just a dream. Horsemen came thundering into the circle of firelight and dust rolled over both fire and the men surrounding it. They stared down with hate at the still form on the ground.

"So he got this far, did he? The bastard!"

No answer from the men at the fire or from the tall, gaunt old one who seemed to be in charge of them.

"We'll take him, then. And we'll hang him from the first damn tree we find."

"No, señor." This was the tall one speaking, calmly, but with a touch of steel in his ancient voice.

"What the hell you talkin' about, Mex? Sure we'll take him. He killed my brother three days ago. What do you care, anyhow? He's dead ain't he?"

"Si, señor. He is dead. And he will be buried with fitting respect, no matter what he has done." The old voice was harsher now, and anger had crept into its cadences.

"You damned spick!"

In the dream, there was a stir of motion from the men around the fire. There were metallic clicks from the hammers of many guns. And there was the old voice again, this time thick with fury.

"Go now, señores, before there are more dead bodies on the ground. This is Grandee, and I am Sandoval Robles. These are my vaqueros. If one of you is foolish enough to touch a gun or speak again, you will all be buried here."

After a time, all was quiet in the dream. It ended as hands once again touched him, stripping the shirt from him and cutting his underwear. There was softness beneath him, the reek of whisky, and after that an unaccustomed tightness around his ribs. When he woke it was broad daylight.

He was alone, on his back, staring up at a sky unbelievably blue. He started to sit up, felt the im-

mediate stab of pain in his wound and grunted sharply.
He heard movement, and a moment later the old one
was above him, staring down.

He tried to sit up again, and this time he made it.
But he had to sit very still for several moments before his vision cleared. He felt the bandage with one
hand.

The old one said, "We have sent for a wagon, señor,
with which to take you to Grandee."

Grandee. The name he remembered from the dream.
Then it could not have been a dream at all. He asked
hoarsely, "Have they gone?"

"The ones pursuing you? Si, señor, they have gone
and will not come back."

"Why'd you do it?"

The old man shrugged, and smiled wryly. "Pride, I
suppose. I do not like names like 'Mex' and 'spick.' "

"Have you got anything to eat here?"

"Of course, señor." The old man turned and said
sharply, "Miguel, our guest is hungry now."

Miguel was squat, dark and heavyset, with straight
black hair that hung to his shoulders and was tied,
Apache style, with a wide band of cloth. Jason
supposed he was either all Indian or mostly so. But he
smiled a broad, toothy grin at Jason and gave him a
plate of highly spiced pinto beans and a tin cup of
steaming coffe.

The spicy smell of beans brought back Jason's
nausea, but he ate in spite of it and after a while the
nausea began to pass. Then he gulped the coffee grate-
fully. He felt weak and sick, but the food and the sleep
he'd had would strengthen him.

The old man squatted across from him and watched him eat. He said, as Jason finished the last of the coffee, "I am Sandoval Robles, señor. This is Grandee and you are welcome here."

Jason stuck out his hand. "I'm Jason Mellor. I owe you my life."

Robles smiled. He must have been seventy or older, thought Jason, but he was as strong as rawhide. He said, "I know you, señor. I saw you once in Santa Fe, though I did not recognize you last night."

Jason said, "You've a right to know what they were chasing me for."

Robles shrugged. "It is not necessary."

"For me it is. I tried to avoid that quarrel back there. But there's always someone wondering whether he can beat Jason Mellor to the draw. Burt Nordyke was one of them. I tried to talk him out of it."

Robles watched him intently. Jason looked up and met the old man's eyes steadily. He had the strange feeling that Robles had taken every word he said at face value.

At last, after studying him for a long time, the old man said, "You are weary of your life, are you not, señor? You would like to see it changed?"

Jason nodded, with some surprise, but he didn't speak.

"So you are running from it. And it follows you."

"Maybe." Jason scowled.

"Grandee is large. Large enough to hide a man."

"Why are you offering me this?"

Robles said, "There are those who would take parts of it for themselves, and who would kill me if they could. Grandee is a grant from the Spanish king, but I am afraid the American courts will support whoever holds possession of it.''

''And you intend to keep possession.''

''I do.'' The implacability of steel was in the old man's voice.

''And you need fast guns.''

''Not exactly, señor. I need men of courage who are practiced in the use of firearms. But most of all I need men who are loyal. And men who can do more than shoot a gun, men who can think. I am offering you a job.''

''After talking to me for five minutes?''

Robles smiled. ''Do you think I am a fool? You have a reputation that is known.''

Jason said, ''I don't know.''

''Consider it, then. Consider also the advantages to yourself. No one challenges a man of Grandee without challenging all of Grandee. You could find something here you have found nowhere else—an end to being alone, an end to personal challenges.''

Robles turned his head as a wagon creaked into camp. It was piled high with blankets. He said, ''In the meantime, you are my guest.''

Jason let Robles and Miguel help him into the wagon bed. The exertion and movement made the world reel before his eyes. He lay back and closed them, and the jolting, excruciatingly painful ride began.

It might have been sleep that possessed him all the way to ranch headquarters or it might have been unconsciousness. In any event, he did not open his eyes until they lifted him from the wagon in the huge courtyard at Grandee.

There were many faces around him—young, old, American, Spanish, and Indian ones. The faces were filled mostly with curiosity, but a few also held compassion.

They carried him into an enormous room, across it and up a short stairway. Thence they went down a wide hall and into another room almost at its end, where they laid him carefully on a bed.

There was a woman here, a young woman whose skin was golden from the sun but whose ancestry was unmistakably American, for her eyes were the clearest blue. Her eyes held Jason's both tenaciously and reluctantly until Robles, beside her, spoke.

"Señora Robles, Señor Mellor. My wife." He spoke a few words to her in Spanish, relating the circumstances that had led to Jason's being brought here, then smiled apologetically at him. "Pardon me for speaking Spanish."

Jason smiled weakly. "I understand it."

There was something about this that was almost too good to be true, he thought. A true Spanish grandee and his beautiful American wife. Robles seemed to possess a quality of gentleness rarely encountered, yet beneath it was the hardest steel. There had to be. Jason remembered suddenly the dream he'd had last night, the dream that was no dream. He remembered Robles' voice as he told Jason's pursuers coldly that if they touched a gun or spoke they would all be buried there. He was certain Robles had spoken the exact truth. Nordyke and his friends had apparently realized it too, for they had gone away without another word.

Uneasiness touched him. Robles certainly did not take in all strangers as he had taken Jason in. He did not bring every wounded saddle tramp and gunman who rode onto Grandee into his house. Why me, then, Jason wondered.

Señora Robles gently shooed everyone from the room, save for a dark-faced woman whom she addressed as Elena. Together the two got his clothes off and Elena washed him as though she had done this kind of chore many times. The señora stood at the window looking out until Elena had finished. Then she returned and helped Elena cut away the bandages.

Jason watched the señora speculatively as she did. She was young enough to be Robles' granddaughter, he decided. And in a way she reminded him of Edie. She had the same dark brown hair, the same clear blue eyes, and an odd little way of smiling, as though her thoughts were far away. The señora had held his glance tenaciously at first, but now she avoided it.

His uneasiness returned. He had a sudden inner certainty that here on Grandee there would be violence, and hatred, and death. Not altogether because he had come or might stay, but because it was inevitable.

Sandoval Robles' action in defending him from Nordyke and his friends, his bringing Jason here, his offer of a job, were things that not only created a debt Jason must pay. They were also proof of Robles' knowledge that trouble was coming to Grandee.

But here, Jason thought, his life might change.

They finished putting salves on the wound, and rebandaged it. Jason closed his eyes with exhaustion as they tiptoed from the room. He slept almost immediately.

It was not an easy sleep. Dreams haunted him, unpleasant dreams of violence and death. Edie was in those dreams, but always so far from him that he could not quite make out her face. And between them stood a line of men with guns, like a wall that Jason must tear down before he could get to her.

Then, when he did get close, he saw it was not Edie at all but Señora Robles instead.

He slept much during the next three days. He ate everything they brought him. And because his body was strong and hard, because the bullet had struck no vital organs, he healed rapidly and soon regained a part of his strength. On the fourth day he got up, as dawn filled his window with gray, and put on his clothes, which had been washed, ironed and mended before they were returned to him.

His head spun crazily with the weakness brought on by exertion. But he determinedly strapped on his gun and belt and went to the window, where he stared out at the vast gray plain.

He owed Sandoval Robles his life. He owed him something more than the theft of his young wife. But if he stayed another day in this room. . . .

Something flowed between them whenever she was here. Something that had been growing with the passing days. Unspoken. Unacknowledged. But something growing like a grass fire fanned by the wind. Something that would be irresistible when his full strength had once again returned.

Moving softly so as to wake no one, he went down the stairs, crossed the enormous living room and went out into the courtyard.

He did not know whether he would leave or stay. He wanted a horse beneath him once again. He wanted to ride across the plain, to be alone with his troubled thoughts.

A young Mexican boy, barefooted, came running with a horse before Jason had been in the courtyard more than a few minutes. Jason thanked him and swung weakly to the saddle. He reined the animal out the gate and rode away toward the north as the sun, rising, stained the thin, high clouds pink.

The answers he had to have would come to him. When he returned, he hoped he would know what he was going to do.

Chapter 4

For a time he rode aimlessly in a general northerly direction. He kept thinking that, so far as the world was concerned, he was dead. Nordyke and his friends would waste no time spreading the news that they had killed Jason Mellor. It would be weeks, perhaps months, before the news that he was alive and here on Grandee got out.

When it did, of course, he would have Nordyke to reckon with, if the man's hatred had not cooled off by then. But for now . . . staying here, he could at least forget for a little while the reputation attached to his name. He could be just another man, working for a wage.

Perhaps if he stayed far from ranch headquarters and from Señora Robles. . . . Yet he knew that would not be possible. Sandoval Robles was not hiring him to do vaquero's work. He was hiring him for his gun.

The miles fell behind and still Jason kept his horse pointed north. A light frown stayed on his forehead and his eyes remained undecided. Weariness increased in him, bringing with it a weakness that was wholly unfamiliar to him. The sun, high in the sky by now, beat against him pitilessly. Rising heat waves made the land waver before his eyes.

He had come too far, he realized. He had overestimated his strength. He started to turn his horse. . . .

He thought it was a mirage at first, but he stopped his horse to stare at it. It looked like a grove of cottonwoods with a small white house standing in their midst.

He moved his head and peered. Nothing changed, moved or disappeared. He reined toward it and touched his spurred heels to the horse's sides. The jolting movement hurt so that he slowed the horse to a walk. He stared at the house, squinting against the glare.

It was the kind of house Edie had always wanted, he thought with mild bitterness, and what he had never given her. It was irony for him to come upon it now, when his thoughts were so strongly upon Edie and the past.

As he approached, the rear door opened and a woman came out. She carried a basket into the yard and put it down, then began to hang out washing on a line strung between two thick-trunked cottonwoods.

He continued to approach, a strange kind of uneasiness touching him now. Something within him urged that he turn around and return immediately to Grandee headquarters, no matter how tired or weak he felt.

Her back was toward him. He rode to within a hundred feet of her and stopped. His breath seemed

caught in his throat. There was a tightness in his chest.
He said, "Ma'am . . ."

Startled, she whirled. There were clothespins in her
mouth, and both surprise and terror in her eyes.

Then he understood the compulsion that had touched
him upon seeing her—the compulsion to return to ranch
headquarters at once. He had recognized her then,
though recognition had been vague and not completely
conscious. It was Edie. It was his wife.

Her voice was a breathless whisper, "Jason!"

He neither moved nor spoke, just stared at her.

She was older, though the years had been kind to her,
showing themselves neither in heaviness nor lines but
only in a rich maturity. Yet there was something in her
eyes—not bitterness, but rather disillusionment. They
were the eyes of a woman who does not expect too
much, either of the world or of the people inhabiting it.

As though in a daze, he dismounted from his horse.
He stumbled from weakness, caught himself and
moved toward her.

Seeing him stumble, her face immediately showed
concern. But it changed at once to an expression of
fatalistic bitterness. She said softly, "You've been
wounded. In a gunfight, I suppose."

He nodded, wanting not the smallest lie between
them now.

"Then you haven't changed."

He said, "Who ever really changes, Edie? I'm the
same man I was before. I carry the same name. But it is
worse now because that name is better known. I don't
often get paid for the use of my gun these days. I'm
forced to use it to stay alive."

She said, "I've changed. I'm not the same woman I was when I was married to you."

"You're still married to me."

"Legally I suppose I am. I don't know how you found me, Jason, but I'm not coming back with you. Not that you'd want me now."

He felt weakness overcoming him. He said, "Mind if I sit down?"

"Of course not." Compassion touched her face, softening it, taking away most of its bitterness and disillusionment. Then it disappeared.

He walked to one of the cottonwoods and sat down at its base, leaning back against the trunk. Edie left her clothesline and came over to stand nearby.

He stared up at her, his face gaunt and drawn. She was a beautiful woman, he thought, even more beautiful than she had been before. Her body was a strong, rounded woman's body, perfectly proportioned, clad today in a pale blue cotton gown. The top button had come undone as she worked, revealing a strong, white throat and the swell of her breasts beneath.

Almost hastily, as though to forestall his asking the same question of her, she asked, "What have you been doing, Jason? And where have you been?"

He said slowly, "It has been no different than when we were together, Edie. I work a while at a riding job, until . . ." He stopped looked directly at her face and then turned away. He said wearily, "Someone always shows up to try me out. Then I have to leave because he has family or friends. But I guess I bought this bill of goods the day I first strapped on a gun. I'm stuck with it."

"Haven't you even tried to change?"

"Of course I've tried. I've grown a beard and worn different clothes. I've been east, and farther west, and north and south. Sometimes I've stayed as long as half a year before someone recognized me. But it never lasted longer than that."

"Well, come in, Jason, and I'll give you something to eat. I can do that much. Are you just passing through?"

"I'm staying on Grandee."

Her eyes widened and color faded from her face. He wondered why. Then she was stooping, helping him up, and her clean woman fragrance was mingling in his nostrils with the smell of strong laundry soap that was still on her hands.

Close to her, his arm across her shoulders, he suddenly wanted all the things she represented in his mind. A home. Roots in the ground that could never be torn out. An end to the aching loneliness of his life. An end to the violence and death that regularly punctuated it.

He wanted to hold her in the darkness of night, to feel her soft warmth beside him when he slept. He wanted to talk his problems out with her and know her compassion and her trust.

The house was cool after the blazing sun outside. He sank into a chair at the kitchen table. The smell of laundry soap was stronger here. On one side of the kitchen was a bench on which were two laundry tubs, one filled with suds and holding a washboard, the other filled with clear water for rinsing.

More water was heating on the stove in a large copper washboiler. But coffee was there too, and Edie immediately filled him a cup and brought it to him. There was a shine of tears in her eyes as she said, "Why couldn't it have been different, Jason? Why?"

He shook his head. "I don't know. But maybe now. . . ."

"No! I won't even think that way. It's over. Too many things have changed since I ran away from you. I have changed . . . and so have you."

"You're still my wife."

"Only in name." There was coldness suddenly in her voice and she wouldn't look at him. "I don't want you, Jason. I don't want to run from place to place. I don't want to lie with you out on the hard ground, or freeze at night, or bake by day. I don't want to ride a horse again or cook over a campfire. And I don't want to listen to gunfire in the streets and wonder whether you will walk back to me or they will carry you."

He gulped the scalding coffee. Something was aching in his chest. He said softly, "All right, Edie. All right."

She looked at him with brimming eyes. "I don't want to hurt you, Jason. But neither do I want to be hurt myself. It wasn't easy to run away from you, but it was easier than staying. It was easier than always knowing that I might slow you down enough to get you killed."

Jason didn't speak.

She said almost hysterically, "Go away, Jason. Don't stay on Grandee. I don't want you here!"

Jason got up. She was shaking violently. Her lower lip trembled and tears streamed across her cheeks. But he didn't touch her. He turned and went out the door.

He had not imagined that their reunion would be like this. He had not imagined that, when he found her, she would still care for him—as so obviously she did.

He wanted nothing so much as to take her in his arms. Yet he knew, with sour bitterness, that doing so would only begin it all again. He would hurt her again, this time worse than he had before. She had built a life for herself here on Grandee. She had roots and peace of mind.

He walked across the yard, feeling her gaze upon his back, swung to his saddle and sat there for a moment, his head reeling, his vision blurring, before he reined away. Only then did he wonder what she did to earn a living out here in this isolated place.

Moodily he rode along, thinking, his eyes fixed on the ground before his horse. Apparently it had not rained here for a long, long time, for the ground was covered with tracks. Horse tracks, mostly, the tracks of shod horses rather than unshod ones. He frowned, turned his head and looked back. Edie was standing in the yard, a tiny figure in a blue gown that whipped lightly against her legs in the breeze. Her arm was up, her hand shading her eyes against the glare as she watched him ride away.

An uneasiness that he did not understand touched him. Something was not right, but he didn't know what it was.

He had gone scarcely more than a mile and had dropped from sight of the house into a small bowl-shaped depression, when he ran into a group of Grandee riders trotting their horses across the land from west to east. When he hauled in, they approached and then stopped fifteen feet away.

One was an American; the others were either Spanish, Mexican or Indian. It was the American who seemed to be in charge. He was grinning oddly at Jason, yet it seemed to Jason that there was both concealed anger and resentment in his eyes. He rode close, stuck out a hand, and said, "I'm Frank Sheets. And you must be Jason Mellor."

Jason nodded and took the hand. Sheets' grin broadened. "Got to hand it to you! Didn't take *you* long to find her, did it? After bein' shot an' all, I wouldn't have thought you'd be huntin' a woman so soon."

Jason's stomach suddenly felt both hollow and very cold. There was a tightness in his chest. He could feel muscles twitching in his arm. "What the hell are you talking about?"

"Sly, ain't you? I'm talkin' about Edie. Who else? Is there more'n one fancy woman out here?"

Jason spurred his horse. The animal jumped, collided with Sheets' mount and bounded away. But not before Jason got a grip on Sheets' throat with both his hands.

As the horses pulled apart, both men were dumped from their saddles. They rolled briefly in the dust. Sheets' face wore an expression of surprise that changed rapidly into one of anger. Jason's eyes burned savagely. In them, for the first time in many months, was the plain compulsion to kill.

Sheets chopped savagely half a dozen times, and Jason's hands relaxed. Breathing hard, his face congested with blood, Sheets rose to his feet. He stared confusedly at the man on the ground, muttered, "Now what the hell got into him? I was only tryin' to be friendly. To hell with him!"

He swung to his saddle and started to ride away. Then he turned and said curtly, "Put him on his horse,

Sanchez, and take him to the house. The old man wouldn't like it if we left him here like this.''

He went on, riding away at a gallop, and disappeared over the rim of the shallow bowl. All the others, but Sanchez followed, raising a cloud of dust behind. Sanchez got off his horse, caught Jason's mount and led him back. He squatted comfortably on the ground while he waited for Jason to come to.

When Jason opened his eyes, a sober-faced Sanchez said, ''Bueno, señor. You are all right, then. Señor Sheets left me behind to take you home.''

Jason scowled and sat up. He looked at Sanchez and quickly looked away. When he licked his lips he tasted blood. He got to his feet with difficulty, not surprised when Sanchez did not offer to help. Stumbling to his horse, he laboriously hoisted himself into the saddle.

Sanchez said, ''I am José Sanchez. I will ride back with you.''

Jason nodded. ''Thanks.'' He was sick from the fight with Sheets. He was weak and his wound was bleeding again. But worse than his sickness of body, worse than weakness, was the nausea that crawled in his mind. Edie had said that she had changed. Several times she had said he would not want her now.

He had wondered how she made her living here, had wondered at the many trails of shod horses leading to and from her house. Now he understood. And he wished they both were dead.

Chapter 5

A moody bitterness of spirit worse than anything he had ever experienced before possessed Jason during the following week. He was weak, but he forced himself to be up at dawn every day. He ate all he could hold, and more, and rode the days away on the wide range of monstrous Grandee. Sandoval Robles, when they met, watched him with speculation in his eyes.

Jason rode south, and east, and west, but never north again. Several times he was caught far from the house at nightfall, and spent the night sleeping under the stars, as he so often had before.

And Clare Robles watched him too, unobtrusively and secretly, her eyes both troubled and confused.

Sheets, Jason learned, was foreman of Grandee, and stayed at the home place in a small room off the gallery surrounding the courtyard. Also at the home place were Jethro, Delehanty, Brown, Moore and Peligan. Except for these six and Jason himself—if he stayed—

the crew of the Grandee was composed of Spanish, Mexican and Indian vaqueros.

Jason himself was given a room several doors down the gallery from that of Sheets, because he refused to stay longer in the house. A dozen times during the week he decided he would leave. A dozen times he reversed himself and decided he would stay. But still he didn't know, and indecision angered him.

If he left he would find his life exactly as it had been before. He would have to move from place to place, withdrawn, friendless, hoping his indentity remained unknown. He would know hunger, and cold, and there would be other Burt Nordykes along the way.

If he stayed, perhaps all that could change. Grandee was a small kingdom in itself. But he must live with the knowledge that Edie was here, that she was being visited by all the Americans working for Grandee, by some of the vaqueros, by others from beyond the borders of Grandee. And there was Clare; there was the unspoken thing growing between the two of them, something that could strengthen because of Edie and his bitterness, but which must not be allowed to strengthen, or even to exist at all.

Today he rode west from Grandee, toward an area he had never seen before, an isolated, grassless country that was a veritable badlands. He did not see the horse of Sandoval Robles following, so far behind that it would have appeared to him only as a moving speck.

He was stronger now. His wound had healed, though it was still scabbed and easily hurt. He had gained back a part of the weight he had lost.

Gaunt and angry, he was, today, a man running and afraid, not of death but of the frightening inevitability of his life. He knew that, had he the recklessness to seize it, his chance of changing it lay here. Here, where existed the wreckage of his previous life. Here, where was his only promise of a future.

Yet if he stayed he would betray the man who had saved his life. He knew that surely and without doubt.

Shortly after noon he entered the badlands, which he had heard called Diablo Canyon. It was a deep, arid gash in the grassy plain, a wasteland of eroded spires and plateaus that stretched for miles and ended at the Diablo River, the western boundary of Grandee.

He wound through its arid miles until he reached the river, and stopped here to stare at the far side. He put his horse into the shallow river and started to ride across.

What stopped him, he didn't know—but something did. He halted in midstream and turned his head, as though listening for some faintly heard sound to be repeated from behind. Then, suddenly, his decision was finally and irrevocably made. He turned his horse and headed back.

There were a score of ways he could have returned. Diablo Canyon was a maze of twisting passageways that led between its eroded spires. What made him choose the one he did? It was aimlessness, perhaps. Or unconsciousness traveling toward the source of a sound so faint he didn't even realize he had heard it.

Before he had gone a mile he saw the first of the buzzards wheeling far up in the flawless sky. They wheeled and plummeted down. . . . He found Sandoval Robles lying on his back, face upward toward the pitiless rays of the afternoon sun. Robles' eyes were closed, his right leg twisted as though it might have been broken by the fall from his horse. There was a broad stain on his chest, gleaming and coagulated, on which several shiny green-black flies were crawling.

Jason halted his horse, took a moment to scan the surrounding country, then swung down and knelt at the old man's side. From the location of the wound he knew Sandoval Robles could not live more than a few moments at most. He was surprised that the old man had lived at all. Robles' chest still rose and fell, but faintly, and its movement was irregular and spasmodic.

Jason said, "It's Mellor, Mr. Robles. You want to say anything?"

Robles opened his eyes and squinted against the glare. Jason moved quickly so that his body shaded them. Sandoval Robles' tall body seemed even gaunter in helplessness than it had before. His dark face twisted with pain and beads of sweat stood out on his forehead. His eyes, seeming almost black as they focused on Jason's face, were touched with immediate recognition.

Jason said, "Do you know who it was?"

Robles shook his head negatively. Jason persisted, "Any ideas?"

Again Robles shook his head. He licked his dry, cracked lips and Jason wished he had carried a canteen. He waited, because there was nothing he could do. Moving Robles would kill him instantly.

Pity touched him. Here was a helpless giant, dying, unable even to name the one who had caused his death. The dulled eyes watched Jason steadily. When it finally came, the voice was cracked and scarcely audible.

"I know about your wife, Mellor. Are you going to run away from it?"

Jason scowled, but he knew this was no time to take offense at the truth. He said, "I *was* leaving. But I changed my mind."

There was approval in the dying eyes. This time his voice was even weaker than it had been before. "Take over Grandee. Keep it in one piece . . . for Clare . . . for my son."

"Son? I didn't know you had one."

The old eyes closed. Jason noted that Robles' chest still rose and fell. He said, "Why me? Why not your son?"

"Because you can do it and he can't . . . or won't."

A spasm touched Robles' face, a spasm of either physical or mental pain. He opened his mouth to speak again, his eyes clinging with a kind of quiet desperation to Jason's face. Then the eyes closed. His last breath came out with a gusty sigh.

It was hard for Jason to believe that this old man was dead. For nearly seventy years he had ridden these wide and empty lands. He had fought wars and skirmishes to keep his property, and his blood was mixed liberally with the land. Seeing him die was like seeing one of the towering sentinel rocks that dotted its reaches disappear like a puff of smoke into the arid air.

Jason stood up and studied the ground around the body carefully. The old man had scarcely moved from where he fell. Jason noted his horse's tracks and the direction from which he had been traveling. Robles had been following him; this was a source of mild surprise.

Kneeling beside the body, Jason turned it over. He noted where the bullet had entered, high below the right shoulderblade, and where it had come out.

He calculated roughly from this information the

location of the ambusher, then mounted his horse and rode that way, up the steep, crumbling hillside north of the place where the body lay. It took him no more than five minutes to find the ambusher's trail, but finding it told him little more than he already knew. Tomorrow he'd come back and follow it out.

Not that he expected much from doing so. The trail would either lead into town and be lost in the streets, or it would be hidden on rocky ground or in a stream someplace.

He dismounted beside Robles' body. A couple of buzzards had already swooped low to alight. They squawked at him and rose, flapping thunderously. He lifted the body and laid it across his horse's rump, securing it with his rope so that it would not slide off. Then he mounted and rode east toward Grandee.

He had grown to like and respect the old man in the few short days he had known him. He also owed Robles a debt. Anger smoldered in him at the way Robles had been murdered—from behind, and for no apparent cause.

But Robles had feared something like this, or else he would not have tried to surround himself with a core of Americans who were efficient with their guns.

Who? One of the ranchers on the perimeter of Grandee? It was the best guess, Jason knew, until there was something better to go on. They probably figured that, with Robles dead, the force with which he had held Grandee for so long would disappear. They could drive their cattle in. Neither Clare nor Robles' son could stop them. And the hired gunfighters wouldn't care.

Jason scowled to himself as he followed the old man's trail eastward toward the mouth of Diablo Canyon. He noticed that the old man's horse was ahead of him, holding its head to one side and trailing the reins, traveling at a steady trot.

How in the devil had Robles found out about Edie being Jason's wife? How, unless Edie herself had told him?

Thinking of Edie was a bitter thing for Jason because he could remember how she had once been. Her eyes had been fresh, and young, and had looked at him with pride—pride that gradually faded as they ran from town to town, that faded with hardship, and hunger, and Jason's broken promises.

And when she ran away he would have followed her, except for the fact that he was on the run himself. He shook his head angrily. He would stay; he had decided that. He would stay and, if it were possible, would do what Sandoval Robles had asked of him.

It was full dark, late, when Jason reached the house. A few dim lights burned in it, and beyond, in the adobe houses that were separated from the main house by a small stream called Caballo Creek. A dark-faced Mexican boy ran barefooted to take Jason's horse, saw its double burden and stopped in terror.

Jason said, "Go into the house and tell the señora that I am here. Tell her I have brought Señor Robles home."

He dismounted wearily. Lanterns hung on either side of the courtyard gate and over the main entrance of the house. He loosened the rope he had used to secure Sandoval Robles' body, coiled it and hung it over his saddle horn. When he saw Clare in the doorway of the house, he quickly slid Robles' body off the horse and into his arms so that she would not see it in such a shocking position.

He walked toward her, carrying it. As she ran toward him he said softly, "It is your husband, señora. He is dead."

She stopped as though forcibly halted by some material thing. Elena, who had followed her out, caught her arm and held it, as though fearing that she might faint.

But her voice, though it trembled, was both controlled and soft. "Bring him in, Jason. Please bring him in and lay him on his bed."

She turned and walked back into the house. Jason followed, turning sideways as he went through the door. He followed Clare across the enormous living room and up the short stairway. He carried Robles into his room and laid him on the bed, not missing the fact that this was strictly a man's room that contained no single thing of Clare's.

He turned and said gently, "I don't know who. . . . He was shot from behind. I found tracks, but there was no time to follow them. Tomorrow . . ."

"Thank you, Jason." It was apparent that she was keeping herself under control by the greatest effort. He found himself wondering what her relationship with Robles had been. Certainly it had not been a conventional man-and-wife thing, yet it was obvious she had thought a great deal of her husband.

He said, "He talked a bit before he died."

"Did he say who?"

Jason shook his head. "He wanted to keep Grandee

intact for you and his son. He asked me to take over and keep it that way."

There was immediate suspicion in her eyes that she glanced away to hide. It came as no surprise to Jason. Such an unusual request by a dying man, unverified. . . .

He said, "We'll talk about it tomorrow. You're his widow, and it will be your choice." His voice was cold in spite of his efforts to keep it from being so.

"Jason, I'm sorry. I didn't mean . . ."

He watched her, feeling the strong pull of attraction. But he didn't speak.

Her face flushed faintly. Her eyes were clear and honest as she met his own. "I want you to know, Jason. I was . . . married to him but we. . . ." She stopped, her flush deepening.

"You don't have to tell me this."

"Oh, but I do. Let's not lie to ourselves, Jason."

He said, "I was leaving partly because of you. But I came back, and that's when I found him."

Her face clouded. She looked at the body of her husband on the bed and tears sprang to her eyes. Without turning she murmured. "Go away, Jason. There is only death for you here. No one can hold Grandee together now that he is gone. They will move in on us from all sides, and they are too many for us to fight."

He said, "Maybe," He waited a moment and then added, "Suppose they do move in? What will happen to the vaqueros and their families?"

"They'll be driven out."

"And you?"

She glanced around at him, suddenly seeming very vulnerable and very young. Jason said, "They'll leave you something this time. But how about the next time they decide to take a bite? And the next?''

''I intend to fight them Jason. As long as I'm able to.''

''I think that's what he would want you to say. And I think I owe it to him to help all I can.''

Gratitude mingled with fear in her eyes. Her hair was down, tumbling across her shoulders. She was dressed for bed and wore a wrapper over her nightgown. He wanted to touch her, but he knew this was not the time.

He turned and left the room abruptly. She followed, and as they walked along the hall and down the stairs he asked, ''What about Sheets? Can you count on him?''

''My husband did.''

''But you don't think you can?''

''I don't know. He's very friendly with some of our neighbors.''

''Do you think he . . .''

''Don't ask me that. There are fifty people who could have shot my husband. No one is well liked who holds as much land as he did.''

Jason headed toward the door. He nodded almost absently at her and went outside. He stood for a moment on the gallery, scowling into the night. He was a fool if he took this on. He could expect support from none of the Americans Robles had hired. Sheets would resent his new position and would probably refuse to stay. The others would probably go when Sheets went, and might even align themselves with the opposition. He would face insurmountable odds.

Nor was he sure why he was trying. Was it for Edie, or Clare, or himself? And, when he faced Grandee's neighbors, would he be fighting them because they were trying to seize Grandee, or because many of them were numbered among Edie's visitors?

Angry and depressed, he watched Sheets hurry toward him along the gallery, buckling on his belt and gun.

Chapter 6

Sheets saw him and stopped. He said, "What the hell . . . has something happened to the old man? Has he been hurt?"

Jason said, "He's dead."

"Dead? He can't be dead. I saw him just . . ." Sheets stopped.

Jason tried to see the expression on his face so that he could evaluate it. If Sheets' words could be taken at face value, the man was genuinely startled at the news. But Jason couldn't see his expression because his face turned slightly away from the light.

He said, "I was leaving. I got as far as the river west of here and turned back. I found Robles in Diablo Canyon."

"Was he dead when you found him? He didn't . . ."

Jason said, "He wasn't dead. I talked to him."

"What'd he say? Did he know who . . ."

"He didn't know. And you didn't know either that

somebody had shot him. For all you knew, he might have been thrown from his horse.''

Sheets took a threatening step forward. "Damn you, you can't . . . "

Jason said sharply, "That's far enough!" and the foreman stopped.

When Sheets spoke again his tone was more moderate. "I've known the old man for a long time and I never knew him to be dumped from a horse. He could only die one way—with a bullet in him."

Jason said, "All right."

"Have you sent for the sheriff?"

"I was going to leave that to you."

Sheets turned. He bawled, "Carlos!" and a few moments later a barefooted Mexican boy about sixteen came running along the gallery. Sheets said sharply, "Ride to San Gabriel and get the sheriff. Take three or four others with you. Tell him I want him here by dawn."

"Señor, it is impossible."

"Tell him that anyway."

The boy turned and ran. Several moments later he thundered out through the gates on a barebacked horse.

Sheets asked, "Did you look for tracks?"

"Uh huh. There wasn't time to follow them, but they'll still be there tomorrow."

"And the killer will be a hundred miles away."

Jason said, "Maybe not. Maybe he'll be right here on Grandee."

Sheets stiffened. "Are you trying to say something, Mellor? If you are, say it and get it over with. I don't know what the hell's biting you, and I'm getting to the place where I don't care. If you think I killed the old man, say so, and I'll damned soon find out if you're as fast as you're supposed to be.''

"Nobody said you killed the old man."

"What'd he say before he died?"

Jason hesitated. Then, knowing there was little point in delaying this, he said, "He asked me to take over Grandee and keep it in one piece for his wife and son."

For an instant Sheets was silent. When he spoke his voice was full of scorn. "For Juan? For Clare? Neither of them's got any right to it. Clare doesn't belong here at all and Juan doesn't give a damn."

"And you do, I suppose."

"I didn't say that. But there are people all around Grandee who are starving for grass. They're the ones who ought to have the land. Clare doesn't need it; a tenth of it would be more than enough for her. It would be all she could manage anyway. And Juan will decorate a scaffold before another year's gone by. Besides, why you? It's nothing to you what happens to Grandee."

"Maybe it is."

"Because of Clare? How many women do you want?"

Jason said, with forced patience, "Sheets, if you don't watch your goddam tongue . . ."

"You're going to have to kill me if you take over here. Or try. And you're going to have to prove that the old man said what you say he did."

"Only to one person, Sheets. His widow."

"And you've already proved it to her. Is that it? Well, maybe I've got a few things to say to the señora myself. Maybe I'll tell her where I found you several days ago. Out at Edie's place. When she finds out you've been beddin' with that whore while she took care of you. . . ."

Jason forgot his wound. He forgot his gun. The word Sheets had put on Edie was like salt in the festering wound of his thoughts.

He launched himself at Sheets. He felt, with solid, exhilarating satisfaction, the hard, brutal impact of his body striking that of the foreman. He groped for Sheets' throat, found it and closed his hands savagely around it.

Sheets bucked like a steer, throwing Jason against the adobe wall of the house. The pair rebounded from that, rolled across the gallery and slammed against one of the ancient posts supporting it.

Sheets broke free, choking, gasping, muttering curses and obscenities. He reached for his gun.

It was almost completely dark out here. The only light was the dimly flickering lantern illuminating the main entrance to the house, and the pair were almost fifty feet from that. In that split second, Jason had a choice to make. Kill Sheets for saying something which, however unacceptable, was true. Or refuse to kill him and try to disarm him instead, risking getting himself killed doing so.

The choice was immediately made, or perhaps had already been made. He sidestepped like a cat as Sheets' gun came up. As the gun blasted, he took a forward step and kicked.

It was almost impossible to see, except that he had the gunflash to guide him. He felt his boot connect with Sheets' extended arm, felt it give and heard the solid thump of the gun on the gallery floor.

Sheets twirled and scrambled toward the gun, grunt-

ing softly and angrily with what must have been
excruciating pain in his arm. Jason followed, and dived
at Sheets just as the man was reaching the gun.

Sheets turned. For an instant the light illuminated his
face. His eyes were narrowed, his lips drawn tight
across his teeth. There was hatred in that face, blind,
implacable. Jason suddenly remembered that out near
Edie's place there had been both anger and resentment
in the foreman's face.

Sheets was in love with her. Jason felt a brief,
reluctant stir of pity for the man. He realized there
could be nothing more degrading or hopeless than a
man's possessive love for a prostitute. There were but
three courses open for such a man—suicide, murder, or
complete degeneration of character.

Yet pity could have no place just now in his thoughts.
Nor could he be very objective in his thoughts of
Sheets, because he also loved Edie, or once had loved
her.

He smashed his fist viciously into Sheets' face, lost
his balance, grappled and smashed the foreman's face
again. Sheets' nose was bleeding profusely, as was his
mouth.

Sheets kept trying to reach his gun: Jason kept
preventing him. A fire was burning in his side and
back, the fire of his reopened wound, but he didn't
care. Tonight it didn't seem to weaken him.

He heard the door open and, though he didn't dare
look, he knew Clare would be standing there. He saw
the vaqueros and their families from across Caballo
Creek streaming in through the gate.

And there was light, from a lamp held by Clare in the

doorway of the house, from lanterns carried by several of the Mexicans.

Jason kneed Sheets in the face as the foreman's hand closed over the barrel of the gun. Sheets fell back, with Jason on top of him. Jason wrenched the gun from the foreman's hand and threw it along the gallery, sliding, for fifty feet.

Sheets broke away and got up. Dragging breath frantically into his starving lungs, he stood glaring at Jason and beyond, looking for something with which he could kill his adversary.

A pile of cobblestones lay at the edge of the gallery; a sledge used to break them lay nearby. Sheets' glance passed over the stones and stopped on the sledge. He lunged toward it.

Jason dived at him. He struck Sheets' body and the foreman fell, but his outstretched hand touched the handle of the sledge. Scrambling forward, Sheets seized it with both hands and, even though he was on his back, he doubled enough to find leverage for a swing.

The sledge whistled past Jason's head. Its momentum nearly tore it from the foreman's grasp. Jason rolled away frantically and got up.

Sheets made it to his feet at the same time and stood crouched, left hand gripping the end of the handle, right holding the shaft high near the heavy steel head. Jason circled him warily, looking for a way to get inside the lethal range of the sledge.

Infuriated as he was, he could still heed the caution that told him one blow, even a glancing one, from that sledge would crush his skull or shatter a bone. He also knew that even if he were crippled, Sheets would finish him off before anyone could interfere.

Circling, he caught a glimpse of Clare Robles standing in the doorway. Her eyes were wide with terror, her lips parted. Frozen there, her eyes were on Jason every minute. He saw her lips form the words, "Please . . . oh God, please!"

Then Sheets rushed, swinging the ponderous sledge as though he were driving spikes into a log wall.

Jason jumped back, saw that it was not far enough, and flung himself to the gallery floor. The sledge whistled close over him, forced down in midswing as Sheets tried to get Jason before he struck the ground.

The sledge's momentum swung Sheets around helplessly, and it was in this split second that Jason sprang at him. He came to his feet in a lunge, hoping desperately that Sheets would not continue his turn and swing the sledge a second time.

Sheets came around, but he was trying to stop and the force of the sledge striking Jason's thigh was considerablly reduced. It was enough to numb the entire leg, to make him stagger, but not enough to stop his charge.

He was inside the range of the sledge now, and had his hands on it. He tore it out of Sheets' hands, raised it to strike, then flung it away disgustedly. While Sheets stared at him with complete surprise, Jason chopped brutally at Sheets' unprotected jaw.

The sound was like that of a cleaver on a butcher's block. Sheets staggered back, his eyes glazing, and Jason followed, chopping mercilessly at the foreman's face.

Even as he did he knew he had no real quarrel with Sheets. The man had simply called a spade a spade and, however distasteful his words might be to Jason, they were still the truth. Nor could he quarrel with Sheets' conviction that Gandee's neighbors had more right to Grandee grass than either Clare or Juan Robles did. It was obviously an honest opinion, honestly held.

Yet looking at Sheets' bloody and twisted face, Jason knew that he had made an implacable enemy.

Sheets stumbled back against the adobe wall of the house. He tried to push himself away from it and only partially succeeded in doing so.

Jason had already begun his swing, and couldn't stop. His fist struck Sheets' jaw and slammed his head back against the wall. The foreman's eyes dulled and his mouth went slack. The expression of hatred left his face and he slid unconscious to the gallery floor.

Jason turned. He was near exhaustion himself and his breath wheezed laboriously in and out of his lungs. He stared at Clare and said harshly, "This was my doing, not his, but one of us has got to go. Make up your mind right now, señora. Do you want me to run Grandee or do you want Sheets to go on with it?"

Her answer was simple and straighforward and given without hesitation, for all that her words were soft. "I want you to run Grandee, Mr. Mellor. It is what my husband wanted, and it is what I want."

He said, still harshly and uncompromisingly, "I will do things you do not like."

She didn't speak, but neither did her glance waver from his. He nodded briefly and turned back to Sheets, who was stirring now. He waited impatiently until the foreman opened his eyes. Then he said, "Get off Grandee, Mr. Sheets. You have until sundown: no longer."

Sheets didn't reply. Jason swung his head to stare at the subdued crowd. "I want ten of the best men on Grandee saddled and ready to ride at dawn. And I want the best Indian tracker we have."

"Si, señor. Si." It came in unison from a dozen throats.

First order of business, Jason knew, was tracking down the killer of Sandoval Robles. After that . . . He frowned. After that the trouble would be coming to him.

Chapter 7

At dawn Grandee was a hive of activity. Messengers rode out in all directions to carry the news of Sandoval Robles' death. The weather was hot and he had to be buried before the day was out. That left barely time for his friends and neighbors to arrive for the funeral.

Also at dawn, Jason rode out, after leaving word that the sheriff was to follow him. Jason wanted to be back in time for the funeral so he could meet the neighbors of Grandee. If possible, he wanted to kill any land-grabbing notions they might have before they gained momentum.

With him were six vaqueros and Jethro and Peligan. Brown and More and Delehanty had elected to quit with Sheets. Jethro was a slim, sandy-haired man about five years younger than Jason. He had reckless gray eyes which held a certain watchful speculation whenever he looked at the new foreman.

Peligan was short, stocky, bowlegged, and looked

more like a sailor than anything else. He was older than
Jason and wore a short, clipped beard liberally
sprinkled with gray. His gun hung in a specially built
holster that fitted into the hip pocket of his pants.

Jason rode at a steady trot, vaqueros and Americans
trailing loosely behind and to both sides of him. The
sun came up and made its steady climb across the sky.

It was almost midmorning before they reached
Diablo Canyon. Jason put his horse down into it, scanning the ground for tracks. He found none until he
reached the place where Sandoval Robles had been
shot.

Jason told Miguel, the man who had given him food
the morning following his escape from Nordyke, to
take up the trail. Miguel nodded, grinned, and headed
along the trail like a hound. He kept his horse at a steady
trot, except in places where the going was too steep.
Jason and the others stayed a hundred yards behind.

The trail left Diablo Canyon by the straightest, most
direct route possilbe, angling north. Jason could see
that the assassin had been pushing his horse hard,
probably in expectation of immediate pursuit.

Out onto the grassy plain went the trail, and now the
fleeing ambusher began to take pains to hide it, or at
least to slow down anyone who might be following. As
Jason had done when fleeing from Nordyke, this
fugitive sought out the canyons with their carpets of
needles, the rocky slopes, the streams. But Miguel
apparently never missed a print.

Noon came and passed. The trail continued inexorably in a northeasterly direction. Jason had not
ridden this way after that first time, when he discovered
Edie's place.

A puzzled uneasiness touched him. Not Edie! He couldn't believe that. She would have no reason to kill Robles: and, besides, he knew her hatred of violence and killing.

While yet several miles from Edie's house, Jason saw the cloud of dust. He frowned and squinted against the glare, because at first he didn't understand what he saw. And then he did, for there were the dark shapes of cattle streaming across a high point of land.

He glanced aside at Peligan, who was also watching the moving herd, and said, "They didn't lose any time."

"Maybe they're Grandee cattle."

"And maybe not. Nobody would be moving that many Grandee cattle this time of year." Jason frowned. "Somebody must have known about Robles' death last night. These cattle had to have been started at dawn today to be this far onto Grandee by now."

The cattle streamed east, passing Edie's place between Jason and the house. At the edge of the trail they had pounded into the sod, Miguel stopped and waited until Jason caught up.

Jason said, "Go on, Miguel. We'll catch up with you."

Miguel nodded. He crossed the cattle trail and quested back and forth beyond it until he found the tracks again. He continued, still at a steady trot.

Jason stared after the cattle herd. Dust rose thickly behind them, but through it he could count half a dozen men. He had seven besides himself. He said, "Come on," and lifted his horse to a lope.

The cattle moved along at a fast, forced walk. Their drovers rode back and forth at the rear and flanks of the herd, yelling, slapping their boots with the ends of their reins.

The drovers saw Jason coming with his men and grouped hurriedly together. They waited this way, while the cattle stopped and began to graze.

Americans mostly, Jason saw as he drew closer. Without taking his eyes from the group, he said, "Know any of 'em, Peligan?"

"Uh huh. It's Roth, from the west side of the Diablo River. The Garcia brothers are with him, and his neighbors on both sides, Lane and Zeitz. The other one works for Roth."

"Which is Roth?"

"The big one in the middle."

Less than two hundred yards now separated the men. Jason stared at Roth.

There was arrogance apparent in him, even at this distance. A man with a monstrous chest and a mane of hair that stuck out untidily and fell long enough to mingle with his beard, he sat his saddle like a rock. Below the hair and above the beard his eyes peered out, shrewd, hard, calculating. There was no fear in the man at all, or if there was it didn't show. Nor was there any uncertainty—only a kind of overbearing contempt.

Peligan muttered, "What're you going to do?"

"Get them off Grandee." He swung his head to glance at the others, at Jethro and the vaqueros. "Keep your guns handy."

He hauled his horse to a halt a dozen yards from the drovers and said, "You're trespassing."

"Who the hell are you?"

"Mellor. I'm the new foreman of Grandee."

"And you think we're trespassing." Roth's voice

was low and hoarse. It was touched with anger, too. "I'll tell you who the goddam trespasser is—Robles and Grandee."

"You know Robles is dead. If you didn't you wouldn't be here."

"Dead, is he? I didn't know, but I'm sure as hell glad to hear it."

Jason said deliberately, "You're a liar, Roth."

Roth's right hand twitched. Then it steadied and gripped his thigh like a claw.

Jason asked harshly, "Who told you Robles was dead?"

"You did. Just now."

"Then you knew he was going to be killed, and who the killer would be."

Roth laughed bitterly. "I can name you fifty men who hated him enough to kill him. This is the United States, mister, not some goddam province of Spain. Good Americans for two hundred miles around are hurtin' for graze while all this goes to waste."

Jason said, "Turn these cattle around and get them off Grandee."

"No! You can go to hell!"

Jason said, "Peligan, go kill ten head of cattle."

This time Roth's hand streaked for his gun, but Jason was ahead of him. He put a bullet into the neck of Roth's horse, then thumbed back the hammer again, prepared to kill Roth if he must. Behind him there was a sudden stir of movement as his men drew their guns or brought their rifles to bear. One of the Garcia brothers clawed for his gun, but a shot from Jethro, over his head, discouraged him. He dropped the gun on the ground.

Roth's horse pitched forward, throwing the big man clear. Roth lost his grip on his gun and it fell to the ground. He stooped ponderously to pick it up. Jason put a bullet into the dust six inches away from it.

Roth froze in a stooped position. His neck, that part of it which was visible, turned dark red. He straightened slowly as Peligan's gun began to bark, then turned and stared unbelievingly while Peligan calmly emptied his gun, reloaded and finished shooting the ten cattle Jason had ordered killed. The others spooked away, bawling at the smell of blood.

Roth turned and stared balefully at Jason, who repeated almost mildly. "Get those cattle off Grandee."

"You dirty son-of-a-bitch!"

"Five more, Peligan." Jason ordered.

"No! We'll get them off!"

Jason repeated coldly, "Five more, Peligan." He waited until Peligan's gun had roared five more times, staring implacably at Roth all the time. Then he said, "Grandee grass isn't going to be cheap, Mr. Roth. It won't be free. But you make up your own mind whether you want to pay the price."

Roth didn't speak. His eyes spoke for him—small, hard, filled with the most vitriolic hatred Jason had ever seen.

He said, "Now drive them off Grandee. Be across the Diablo River before dark."

"We can't. . . . "

Jason glanced at Peligan. Roth screamed, "All right! All right! But you ain't heard the last of this, mister. Before I'm through with you, you'll wish you'd never been born!"

Jethro said cheerfully, "Roth, I'd say you was lucky you ain't dead."

Roth didn't even glance at him. He turned, climbed up behind his hired man and rode toward the cattle, his men following along sullenly behind.

Jason waited until they had started the cattle west. Then he jerked his head in the direction Miguel had gone and rode that way, followed by Peligan, Jethro and the other vaqueros.

Miguel was waiting patiently for him a quarter mile short of Edie's house. As Jason rode up, he pointed toward it. "Trail go there, señor."

Jason nodded. "Did you circle the house? Did you find the tracks going away?"

Miguel nodded. "Horse only. No rider."

Jason frowned. He had expected something like this. He doubted if the killer was still at Edie's place; he had simply ridden out on a different horse.

He asked, "How many other trails?"

Miguel held up a hand, the fingers spread.

Five, then. Five trails, any of which might be the killer's. By the time he followed out five trails . . .

He said, "Wait here for me. I'll be back as soon as I can."

Chapter 8

He rode slowly, staring steadily at the house. His eyes were troubled, him mouth grim. Meeting Edie again would be painful for both of them, now that he knew her profession and she knew he did.

He blamed himself, realizing that he was, in a sense, responsible for what she was. He had given her nothing but unhappiness. And yet, he also knew that other women, equally hurt and alone, had supported themselves in other ways.

He did not concern himself about personal danger. He knew that even if the killer were still in Edie's house he wouldn't dare shoot, with seven men waiting in plain sight of the house.

Jason saw Edie come from the kitchen door and stand there, a hand raised to shield her eyes from the sun. She looked so fresh and clean in her gingham gown. . . . His face twisted with a sudden pain.

He nodded, touched the brim of his hat with his hand and said, "Hello, Edie."

"Hello, Jason." She tried desperately to meet his eyes, failed, and glanced down, color rising in her cheeks.

Jason said, "I know, Edie. I know." It was his turn for confusion, but he went on stubbornly, "Damn it, I'm not a judge and you're not on trial. I trailed a man here, a man I want. He turned his horse loose and rode a fresh one away. Who was he?"

She shook her head without speaking.

Jason's voice was harsh. "How many were here last night?"

She glanced up, defiance plain in her expression. "I don't count. Jason, leave me alone. Go away and leave me alone!"

"How many?"

"Five." She could no longer meet his eyes.

He swung from his horse, dropped the reins and walked to her.

She said hurriedly, "Will you have some coffee, Jason?"

"Thanks." He followed her in, feeling the need to touch her in spite of himself. She was still his wife. . . .

He looked inwardly at himself with sour distaste. She had been as fresh and clean as she now looked when he'd first met her . . . He shook his head violently. Who was he to condemn? He had killed, again and again. He had excused himself on the grounds that each killing had been forced on him. Wasn't it possible that Edie's life had also been forced on her?

He said, "I've got no right to ask, but I'd like to know. How . . . "

"How did I get started doing what I'm doing now?" She pulled the coffeepot forward on the stove and turned almost angrily to face him. "We had so little, you and I. Horses. Saddles. The clothes we wore on our backs." She stopped. "What difference does it make? I have no excuses. I'm what I am."

He said, "All right, Edie."

She raised her head spiritedly. "No, it isn't all right. I wanted things. I wanted a clean white house. I wanted to dress like a woman and look like a woman. I wanted to *feel* like a woman. Does that sound so strange to you?"

"No, it doesn't sound strange."

"When I left you, I tried a lot of things. I scrubbed. I waited on tables. And then I met a man. . . ."

Jason said, "Never mind." It shouldn't hurt him to think of her with another man. God knew she'd been with a lot of them. He repeated almost angrily, "Never mind."

"No, I want you to hear. I've heard your excuses for being what you are. Now hear mine for being what I am."

The coffee began to simmer noisily. For the moment, Jason had forgotten Robles' death, had forgotten the trail he had followed here.

Edie said, "I couldn't marry him—I was still married to you. So I ran away with him." Her face grew pale and her mouth trembled. "He took me to a town in Colorado, a mining town that had no buildings, only tents. He brought a bottle of whisky to the tent and made me drink it. Then he took my clothes away from me. After that he left, but he sent men into the tent. I don't know how many of them. A lot of them." She was trembling all over now.

Jason said sharply, "Stop it! I don't want to hear!"

"But I want you to. I think you should. I was sick when I woke up. He laughed at me and he told me how many men he'd sent to me. He showed me the money he'd collected from them."

She began to cry hysterically. Jason wanted to hold her in his arms, yet he didn't move. He felt sick, and dirty, and more angry than he had ever been before in his life.

"It went on like that for more than a week. Then he was killed in a gunfight and I was all alone. Can you understand that, Jason? I was all alone. I'd had most of the men in that camp in bed with me, so I just kept on with it. It was winter and I couldn't travel over the mountains by myself. There wasn't anything else that I could do."

She looked up bravely at his face. She winced visibly. Then anger sparkled in her eyes. It faded gradually.

"I guess I deserved that look, Jason. It's the same look I gave you the day I walked out on you."

Jason said, "The coffee's boiling."

She turned, got the pot, and filled a cup for him. He sat down at the table and sipped it, grateful for anything that would get them off the subject they'd been on. He said harshly, "That man I trailed in here—he's a killer. He murdered Sandoval Robles by shooting him in the back. I want him, Edie. I'll get him. But it will make it easier all around if you'll tell me who he was."

He glanced up at her face. Her eyes were wide with

terror now and her lips were bloodless. She shook her head. "I can't tell you, Jason. I can't. He'd . . ."

Jason nodded. "He might at that. But if you don't tell, he may kill you anyway. If I know who he is I can get him before he gets to you."

Her head continued to shake, and terror did not leave her face.

Jason said, "Maybe you're in love with him. Is that it?"

She shook her head dumbly. Jason got to his feet, took hold of both her arms and shook her. "Edie! He killed Sandoval Robles! Doesn't that mean anything to you?"

Her lips moved, but she didn't speak. Jason stared into her eyes for a moment more, then released her. Standing this close, her clean fragrance in his nostrils. His fists clenched tightly at his sides.

What was it about her? He was sick with thinking of her in the arms of anyone who had the price. And yet, he wanted her so badly that he could scarcely control himself.

He turned furiously and stalked from the house. He stood for a moment beside his horse, fumbling in his pocket for tobacco with hands that shook uncontrollably. Why was life so cruel? He hadn't wanted the life he was forced to live. Edie hadn't wanted the life that had been thrust on her.

He could imagine how she had felt, back in that mining town a hundred miles and a hundred years away. She'd probably known that she could never feel clean again, that no one would want her . . . and she had to live.

She'd had no more control over her destiny than he'd

had over his. He turned as if to go back. Perhaps
together, somehow, somewhere, they could begin
again and forget the past. But he knew they never
could. Every time he touched her he would wonder how
many others. . . .

He swung angrily to his horse's back and thundered
out of the yard without looking around. Yet the impossible dream remained—the dream of a new beginning for the two of them.

Miguel, Peligan, Jethro and the four vaqueros were
waiting where he had left them. He was surprised to see
understanding and sympathy in the faces of two or three
of them.

He said harshy to Miguel, "She knows who he is but
she won't tell. She's scared. So I guess we'll have to
follow out the five trails. Take one yourself and put
your vaqueros on the other four."

"Si señor." Miguel repeated the instructions in
Spanish to the four vaqueros. The five rode away,
scanning the ground, circling Edie's house.

Jason stared at the house for a moment, the things he
was feeling plain in his face. Then he turned his horse
and touched the animal's sides with his spurs. He heard
the other two following along behind.

Edie was in danger. Whoever had killed Sandoval
Robles wouldn't hesitate about killing her. But Jason
couldn't help her until she told him the killer's name.

He forced his mind away from her, forced himself to
think about Robles. Instead he found himself thinking
of Robles' wife. Old Sandoval Robles had been no
fool. He'd known about the attraction between Jason
and his wife. Even if he had never said anything, he had
surely known.

The way was clear now. And though he was ashamed of the thought, Jason couldn't put it away from him. There was no longer a barrier between Clare Robles and himself.

He found himself thinking of what it would be like to hold her in his arms. Angrily he shook his head. There would be time enough for that—if he lived, if he drove back the invasion of Grandee that was sure to come.

Roth had started it. And while Jason had successfully driven him off, he knew he hadn't seen the last of him. The man was infuriated and would be back with a force big enough to insure success next time.

Briefly Jason wondered which side was really right. Had Robles really been entitled to hold so much land, when others needed it so desperately? Was a grant from the Spanish king valid or right, now that this land was part of the United States?

Impatience touched him—impatience with himself. The right or wrong of the grant would be decided by the courts. All he need concern himself with were basic things. Like loyalty to a man who had saved his life, who had offered him a chance to change the pattern of his life.

Jethro and Peligan caught up with him and rode abreast, glancing speculatively at his face. Jethro asked, "What're you goin' to do, Mr. Mellor?"

There was no hesitation in his reply. "We'll do the same as we did earlier today. We'll keep 'em off, no matter how it has to be done. If they want Grandee, they'll have to get it through the courts."

Chapter 9

From a high spot of ground a couple of miles from Grandee headquarters, Jason could see the dust of rigs moving toward it from all directions. There were buggies and surreys and wagons. There were horsemen too. And even from here he could see how crowded was the courtyard in front of the sprawling house.

Sandoval Robles had been an institution, as much so as Grandee itself. He had been a part of the land, solidly entrenched, when the others came. Now they streamed in from the plain to his funeral and Jason knew the motives that brought them were as different as night and day.

Some came out of respect and because they had been Robles' friends. Some came because they were curious. Still others, who wanted his land, came to evaluate the vulnerability of Grandee. Even his enemies came, to gloat, perhaps, or to satisfy themselves that he was really dead, this legend that had endured for so long.

Jason touched spurs to his horse lightly and galloped down the rise. He passed a buggy, neither turning his head nor speaking to the occupants. He led Jethro and Peligan into the courtyard and swung down from his horse. A Mexican boy, barefooted and solemn of face, took the horses and led them away. Jason glanced around.

The air of the courtyard was almost festive, in spite of the black clothing most of the mourners wore. He crossed to the gallery, walked along it to the door, and entered.

Robles' casket rested at the far end of the room. In one corner stood a priest, talking to a group of people. Jason climbed the short flight of stairs and went along the hall to Señora Robles' room. He knocked lightly.

"Come in." Her voice was subdued and scarcely audible. He opened the door.

She was dressed in black and wore a black lace mantilla over her head. Her expression was sombre, but there were no signs of tears. Her eyes clung to his as she said, "Tell me what happened, Jason. Did you find the man?"

He shook his head. "We trailed him to . . . to Edie's place. She knows who he is, I think, because he rode one of her horses away from there. But she refused to tell."

Clare didn't speak. Her gaze rested steadily on his face.

He went on, "There were five trails last night. I put a man on each of them, but I can't promise any results. All five trails will probably be lost in some settlement or other. A lot of time has passed."

"Then your chance of finding the killer isn't very good?"

"I wouldn't say that. Edie will probably talk, sooner or later." He hesitated a moment and then said, "There was something else. We found a man named Roth driving cattle onto Grandee range. He refused to drive them back. There was some trouble."

"I'm sure whatever you did was right."

He grinned ruefully. "From our standpoint, maybe. I had fifteen of the cattle shot, and Roth's horse got shot too. He was pretty worked up when he finally headed home."

He raised his eyes to hers. Something strong and undeniable passed between them. He said, "I think your husband knew about you and me. He was too smart not to have known. And I don't think he was angry, either at you or at me."

She whispered, "I'm sure he knew. Our relationship was not. . . . We had separate rooms, Jason. He loved me and I loved him. But we were not. . . ." She stopped and smiled apologetically. "This is very hard to explain. We were married, but we were not husband and wife."

Jason nodded, wondering why the words brought such a flood of relief to him.

She changed the subject suddenly. "I thought he would have wanted the funeral here. I don't think he would have wanted this place left unguarded, even long enough for the trip into San Gabriel and back."

Jason nodded. He went to the door. "There is something you should know about me. Edie is—was—my wife."

Her expression showed instant compassion. "How terrible for you!"

He shrugged.

She asked, "Are you still in love with her?"

He met her eyes steadily. "No. I could never. . . ." He stopped, knowing that wasn't true, remembering the way he had wanted Edie not three hours past.

Pain touched her face briefly and went away. He finished, "I could never be a husband to her again. There's too much. . . ."

Clare said almost inaudibly, "You didn't have to explain."

He said, "I think I did. Because I wanted you to understand." He stepped out the door and closed it behind him, then stood for a moment in the hall, knowing he had hurt her and sorry because he had.

He had said he wanted her to understand. Yet how could she, when he didn't understand himself? How could a man love two women? He wanted Edie, but he knew getting together with her again would not work. He wouldn't be able to forget what her life had been, any more than she would be able to forget his. And he wanted Clare.

He went along the hall angrily, down the short flight of stairs, and across the enormous room. People were filing in, taking seats quietly or standing with their hats held awkwardly in their hands. Jason lost himself in a far corner of the room where shadows all but hid him, and watched the faces of the people as they came.

He knew only a few of them, but he had a feeling he would know most of them before the issue confronting him was solved.

He saw the sheriff, who was instantly recognizable

by the star he wore pinned to his shirt. Jason studied the man, knowing he would have to deal with him, and wanting to evaluate him first.

The sheriff was a tall man, running to paunchiness although he could not have been much more than thirty-five. He wore a pair of brush-scarred boots from which the spurs had been removed. Plainly he was not dressed for a funeral. He had probably been working when he got the word.

His face was beginning to grow heavy, but there was no weakness in it. Almost ponderous of feature, it held authority and a certain arrogance as well. Here, thought Jason, was a man very sure of himself and his capabilities.

A deputy had followed the sheriff in, slighter and shorter, a man with a deferential air toward his boss. Jason glanced at him and glanced away, unimpressed. The sheriff sat down and his deputy sat beside him. Jason continued to study the sheriff's face.

Dark eyes. Heavy, dark brows. A long, straight nose and a mouth almost hidden beneath a thick mustache but showing strength and determination for all of that. And a deeply cleft chin that was like solid rock.

Gun worn fairly low, Jason remembered, but not tied down. A man who would hit with his first bullet the target at which he shot. But a man who would be slow and deliberate about getting out his gun.

Jason found himself hoping the sheriff would be on his side. But he doubted if he would. The sheriff was an American, and as such would be aligned with the enemies of Grandee. Not that he would allow anything illegal—but his sympathies would be with the neighbors of Grandee who needed grass.

The funeral began. Jason put only part of his attention on it, and continued to study faces. He saw one young man who, he thought, must look as Sandoval Robles had once looked when he was young. And as the thought crossed his mind, his attention sharpened. Could this be Juan? After that, he watched the young man steadily.

The young man's face was haughty and arrogant. The mouth was too soft, too spoiled. The eyes, dark and sensitive, were brooding and angry. His manner was one of impatience.

Surely this could not be Juan, Jason thought. He would not be impatient at his father's funeral, even if the two hadn't gotten along.

It was over at last. Jason watched the mourners file out. The sound of women weeping was plainly audible. He looked for Clare, saw her and realized that she was weeping too.

When the crowd had thinned, the sheriff went out. Jason followed. By now he had lost sight of the young man he had been watching earlier. He approached the sheriff and stuck out his hand.

"I'm Jason Mellor. I take it you're the sheriff."

The man nodded and shook his hand. The grip was strong but not excessively so. The sheriff, Jason decided, didn't have to prove anything, either to himself or to anyone else.

The sheriff said hoarsely, "Les Proust is the name. Glad to meet you. I've been trailing you all day—from the badlands to Edie's place, then back here."

Jason didn't speak, and after a moment Proust went on. "You and your men pretty much messed up what trail there was. Find anything?"

Jason shook his head. "The trail went to Edie's place. Five trails led away. I put a man on each."

Proust nodded. "Then Edie probably knows."

Jason shrugged. He realized that if it was generally spread around that Edie knew the killer's name, the danger to her would be immeasurably increased. He said, "She probably knows it was one of the five."

Proust said, "I'll talk to her."

He studied Jason for a moment, his eyes growing hard. "I found fifteen dead cattle out there, and one of Roth's horses shot. You know anything about it?"

Jason felt his wariness increase. He nodded. "I ordered the cattle shot. Roth's horse was killed when Roth tried to put up a scrap."

"Why?"

Jason smiled thinly. "Ought to be obvious, shouldn't it? The cattle belonged to Roth. It was Grandee range. I ordered him to move 'em off and he refused. It took a little persuasion. He moved 'em in the end."

"You think you're God?" Proust's eyes bored steadily into Jason's own.

Jason met the sheriff's gaze, his own equally hard. He said, "No. I know exactly who I am. I'm the man Señora Robles put in charge of Grandee. I'm the man Sandoval Robles asked to hold it together just before he died. And I'm going to do it, Sheriff, no matter who gets hurt."

"It's a Spanish grant. It's shaky. The courts will probably throw the whole damn thing open."

Jason said, "You know better than that. The courts are likely to support whoever holds the land. So tell your friends all around Grandee that if they want it they'll have to pay for it in blood. I'm going to hold it for Señora Robles, no matter who gets hurt.

The sheriff's eyes were momentarily balked. Then his own anger began to stir. He said, "Ought to be a warrant out for you someplace. I might be able to find it, you know."

Jason grinned mockingly. "Try, Sheriff. Try finding one. And while you're doing it, take a good, long look at your own honesty, because you'll be skirting a problem you can't meet head on. I may be well known, but that isn't the point, is it? The point is that the Robles family owns this land. It belongs to them. And in keeping it for them, I'm doing your job because you don't want to do it yourself."

Proust's face lost color. His eyes glittered. When he spoke, his words came thinly from between clenched teeth. "Murder's a crime, Mellor—on Grandee or any-place else. Keep it in mind."

He glared at Jason for a moment more, then whirled and strode away. His deputy followed, glancing over his shoulder at Jason. The pair mounted and rode at a hard gallop out the gates.

Jason turned away, frowning, He had hoped the sheriff would be on Grandee's side. He had hoped to have help from the law in the battle he knew was sure to come.

Now he knew he could count on no help. Neutrality was the best he could hope for from Sheriff Proust. And in view of the sheriff's parting remarks, he doubted if he could even hope for that.

The first time someone was killed over Grandee grass, Proust would promptly arrest him—or try to. And with Jason gone, with Grandee leaderless, it would be simple for anyone who wanted it to take all or part of it.

He watched gloomily as the casket was loaded into a hearse, watched as the burial procession filed out of the courtyard and headed toward the family burial plot, half a mile away. He watched the mourners who had not joined the procession get into their rigs and leave.

He had faced overwhelming odds before, but the problem itself had always been simple. Survival had always been the issue. This time he would be fighting many battles as he tried to keep Grandee intact. He would be fighting for Clare, for a chance at a future with her. He would be fighting the past, and the things the past had done both to Edie and to him. He would be fighting for a chance to leave behind him the life he now was forced to live.

And, he admitted ruefully, he would be fighting Americans exactly like himself, who felt they were right. That was going to be the hardest part of all.

Chapter 10

For a time, Jason paced the courtyard thoughtfully, trying to plan his strategy. He supposed it would be necessary to send half of the vaqueros on patrol, so that he would know the location of each invasionary thrust. But he would need an adequate force here, too, for Grandee headquarters might be attacked.

He realized there was only one plan of action that would work. He must attack mercilessly any force moving onto Grandee. He must make invasion so costly for those who tried it that others would be discouraged from any attempts.

The course was dangerous, for Proust had threatened him with a murder charge if anyone were killed. But it was the only way that would work. If he tried bargaining, it would be interpreted as weakness, and Grandee would soon be overrun.

Sandoval Robles had undoubtedly anticipated something like what was happening now. He had tried to surround himself with men like Jason, on whose loyalty he thought he could depend. Sheets had taken some of these men with him when he left. Others would leave when they understood the odds against Grandee. But the vaqueros would stay. And so would Jason himself.

He shrugged lightly, but his eyes did not lose their worried look. The next couple of weeks would decide many things—whether Jason would live or die; whether Grandee would remain intact; whether he picked up the old life with Edie, forever on the run, or whether he stayed here with Clare.

He heard the burial procession returning. A horseman rode into the courtyard, glanced around and then approached. It was the young man Jason had noticed earlier. He stared down at Jason arrogantly.

"I am Juan Robles. I guess you're Jason Mellor."

Jason nodded. He studied Juan, noticing things he had not seen before. Robles was dressed in black—tight black pants, fancy tooled black boots, a short jacket, a flat-crowned black hat, and a white shirt. A dandy, Jason thought. A ladies' man.

Robles wore a gun in a tied-down holster. The grips were smooth and dark from wear. Jason's practiced eye told him Juan would be very fast.

Juan said haughtily, "I will be managing Grandee now. You will not be needed. If you will let me know the amount that is due you. . . . "

Jason said softly, "You're mistaken. *I'm* running Grandee. And there will be more to it than watching the vaqueros work."

He did not immediately understand his own irritation. He supposed it was caused, in part, by Juan

Robles' haughty arrogance. But it was also caused by
worry and a nagging thought that he might have taken
on an impossible job.

Robles' reaction to his words was instantaneous. His
face darkened and his eyes snapped with anger. He
swung from his horse. "I repeat, señor—you will not
be needed. Will you leave peacefully or must I. . . ."

Jason grinned. "I don't want to fight with you. Go
talk to Señora Robles. Get it straightened out with
her."

Juan spit on the ground at his feet. "That Yankee
woman? She has no rights here. This is Grandee, and I
am Juan Robles."

Jason said, "This is also the United States."

His irritation was rising. The procession had entered
the courtyard. He saw Clare step from a buggy and
walk toward the house. An elderly man alighted from
the same buggy, looked around, then walked toward
Jason and Juan.

Juan's tone changed, became soft and measured.
"Will you leave, señor? Or will you force me to kill
you?"

Jason calculated the distance between them, knowing it was too great for a sudden rush. He felt the old
tension coming over him, and felt as well a nausea that
rose from a knot in his stomach and filled his throat. He
didn't want to kill Sandoval Robles' son. He par-
ticulary didn't want to kill him here.

Old Sandoval Robles had told him staying would
mean an end to personal challenges. It appeared that
Sandoval Robles was wrong.

The elderly man, halfway to the pair, called, "Juan!
Stop it!"

Juan turned his head. "Stay out of this, Señor Haskell."

No conscious thought prompted Jason. He was in motion the instant Juan's head turned, rushing across the space between them, lunging, for he knew that when Juan glanced back at him he would draw his gun.

Juan's head jerked back. His eyes widened slightly and his hand streaked toward his gun. He was fast, faster even than Jason had believed he would be. The gun was out and up as Jason struck him and knocked him back.

The gun discharged, so close Jason felt the heat of the muzzle blast. The bullet burned his upper arm. Then he had Juan between his hands. He wrenched the gun away and flung it halfway across the courtyard.

He turned back to Juan and clipped him solidly on the jaw. Juan stumbled back half a dozen steps, then sat down. His eyes were murderous and his mouth trembled. For an instant Jason thought he was going to burst into tears.

Haskell reached Jason and touched his arm. "Wait, Mr. Mellor. No more. Let me talk to him."

Juan struggled to his feet, brushing the dust from his clothes. Haskell said, "Señor Robles has asked Mr. Mellor to take Sheets place as foreman, Juan. It is a wise choice. If anyone can keep Grandee intact, Mr. Mellor can."

"And I say he goes. I am Juan Robles, Señor Haskell. Grandee now belongs to me." Juan's voice trembled.

Haskell shook his head. He was a tall, gaunt man, in

his seventies. He wore a trimmed, graying beard and a short mustache. His suit was black, and he was bareheaded.

He said, "Under the law, if a man dies intestate—that is, without making a will—his estate goes equally to his widow and his offspring. Half of Grandee is yours, Juan—but only half."

"Then I have as much to say about him as she does."

Haskell shrugged. "I suppose you do. But no more than she."

Jason stared at the pair. He glanced toward the house and saw Clare watching from the door. Would she support him now? he wondered. Would she risk an open break with Juan over a man she could not bring herself to wholly trust?

She left the door and crossed the courtyard. Her face was white, her eyes troubled. A quarrel now, with the body of her husband scarcely cold. . . . But her chin was firm and her head high as she faced Juan.

"I am sorry, Juan, but I want him to stay. Without him Grandee will fall apart."

Juan said viciously, "Bitch! Faithless bitch! How long before my father died were you and he. . . ."

He didn't finish. Jason's hand swung, and the slap was loud enough to be heard all over the courtyard. Blood trickled from the corner of Juan's mouth and across his chin. Clare winced visibly, but her face lost none of its determination.

Haskell said, "This isn't getting us anywhere, Juan. If you can't speak with respect, don't speak at all. There's only one way to settle this. We'll find out who the vaqueros will take orders from."

"Bueno. Call them." Juan's dark eyes gleamed with triumph.

Jason looked questioningly at Clare. Juan and Haskell moved across the courtyard to gather the vaqueros. Jason stepped close to Clare.

"Didn't he leave a will? It seems unbelievable. . . ."

She shook her head. "He once had one that left everything to Juan. Then Juan and he quarreled, and he tore it up. It wasn't long after we were married that he began to hire men who . . . well, men who were good with guns. He knew trouble was coming, because there were so many newcomers around Grandee. And I almost think he had some kind of premonition that something was going to happen to him."

She stopped. Jason said, "Before or after he quarreled with Juan?"

"I don't know."

There was a great deal of shouting as Juan gathered the vaqueros. They came filing into the courtyard, many of them dressed in their best, which they had worn to the funeral. Behind them came their families, fearful, uncertain.

Juan strode across the courtyard, with Haskell following. He said confidently, "Now ask them who is the rightful owner of Grandee. Ask them if they will follow the gringo woman, or if they will follow me." He took a stand a dozen yards from Clare and Jason, facing them. His gun still lay where Jason had thrown it earlier.

The vaqueros, of whom there appeared to be about twenty, looked from Clare to Juan and back again.

They talked briefly among themselves in Spanish, but
their words were too softly spoken to be understood. At
last they shuffled across the courtyard, past Juan, to
take a stand behind Clare.

For an instant Juan seemed stunned, unbelieving.
Then a dark flush stole across his face. His eyes blazed.
He whirled, strode to his gun and snatched it up. For a
moment it seemed he might use it against Jason, but he
changed his mind and thrust it into its holster.

His back stiff, he stalked to his horse and swung
astride. The animal reared from the cruel gouging of the
spurs and the inflexible tightening of the reins. Juan
quieted him by sheer force. He rode the prancing animal to Jason and stared down furiously.

"I will kill you, señor. I promise you that I will kill
you before a week has passed."

Jason shrugged. He didn't speak, aware that anything he said would probably bring from Juan a tirade
against Clare.

Juan whirled his horse, rearing, again. He sank his
long cartwheel spurs into the animal's sides and
thundered out of the courtyard.

For several long moments after he had gone there
was utter silence. Then the vaqueros began to disperse
uneasily.

Jason said, "I will want to see all of you together in
half an hour."

"Si, señor." The words came from a dozen throats
at once.

Haskell turned to Clare. "Good-bye, señora. If there
is any way that I can help. . . . "

Jason said dryly, "There will be, Mr. Haskell.

Grandee will need the services of an attorney in the next couple of weeks.''

Haskell's expression became grave. "I hope you do nothing unlawful.''

Jason grinned. "We'll hold Grandee by whatever means are needed. If that's unlawful. . . .''

His expression worried, Haskell crossed the courtyard and climbed into his buggy. He drove out.

Clare said, "Have you a minute? Could you come in?''

He nodded, and followed her into the house. She crossed to a window and stood looking out. When she turned, her eyes were frightened. "I'm afraid, Jason. I'm afraid for you. I want you to give it up and go away.''

He stared at her. "You are firing me?''

Her chin firmed. "Yes, Jason, I'm firing you. I want you off Grandee by morning.''

He shook his head. "I won't go.''

She said, "Jason, I'm ordering you to go.''

"I still won't go. Because you don't want me to. And I . . . There's nothing for me unless I stay. I'll go from town to town, leaving someone dead in each one, chased all the way to the next. I can't last that way forever, Clare. Sooner or later someone will be faster than I am. Or I'll do what I nearly did the last time—I nearly didn't draw my gun at all because I didn't want to kill again.''

"But here death for you is certain, Jason. You won't have a chance. There's Juan, and Roth, and a dozen others. All of them know you're the only thing standing between them and Grandee.''

He crossed to her and stood, not touching her, a foot away. He said, "This isn't the time, but there are things to be settled between you and me."

"Yes, Jason."

"So I'll stay. It's the only thing I want. I'd as soon be dead as leave."

She nodded reluctantly. Her eyes were troubled, but there was a faint smile on her mouth.

He said, "I thought I'd put about half the vaqueros out to ride. When they see someone moving in they'll ride back here. We'll have to hit hard and fast at whoever tries to move in. We'll have to hurt them and turn them back. You may not like the things I will do, but there is no other course."

"You are sure it's the only way? The courts . . ."

"Will support whoever holds possession."

"And if that is Juan. . . . Perhaps if I turned Grandee over to him, all this trouble could be averted."

Jason shook his head. "You know better than that. Juan can't hold it. They'd take it away from him in a week, and kill him to boot."

"I suppose you're right."

He stared out the window at the vaqueros gathering in the courtyard. He said, "I'd better get started."

He went outside. They watched him with impassive faces, with watchful eyes. They would do as he asked, but not for him, he knew. They would do it for Sandoval Robles, who was dead. They would do it for Grandee, for their homes. Lastly, they would do it for Clare.

He said, "I want ten men to leave here right away. They will scatter and ride the boundaries of Grandee, and then they ride back here quickly when they see someone moving onto Grandee. The others are to stay.''

He selected ten by pointing them out, because he didn't know all their names. The ten left quickly to get horses and provisions. The others watched him expectantly. He said. "We'll wait. But we will not have to wait long. Keep your guns and ammunition close to you.''

He watched as the ten dispersed excitedly. He had sounded confident. But he knew the odds. If he held Grandee, it would be a miracle.

Chapter 11

The sun sank slowly behind the western plain. In early dusk, Jason saddled a horse and rode out to a high point of ground, from which he stared back at the sprawling city of buildings that comprised Grandee.

There was the main house with its walled courtyard; the small, adobe houses of the vaqueros; the working buildings; and the corrals. There must have been forty or fifty buildings in all. In one sense, he realized, the place was indefensible. And yet, taking it could be a costly business, if the inhabitants were ready and not taken by surprise.

Much depended, of course, upon how large a force attacked. His eyes narrowed slightly. Juan would probably make bargains with Grandee's neighbors. He would trade pieces of Grandee range in return for support. And he would surely be able to enlist Sheets' support, and that of the men who had left with him. He might be able to raise fifteen or twenty men.

There was also Roth. His rage at seeing his cattle shot would not soon cool. He could probably muster a force equal to Juan's. If the two forces moved in at the same time, from different directions. . . .

Shrugging lightly, Jason reined his horse around and headed back. There was little point in creating difficulties in his mind. He would meet each threat as it arose.

It was full dark when he arrived. Scarcely had he entered the courtyard when he heard a horse approaching. Miguel rode in, dismounted from his lathered horse, and handed the reins to the Mexican boy who had run out from the gallery. He approached Jason.

"The trail lost itself in San Jose, señor. That is a little village at the southern edge of Grandee."

Jason nodded. "I expected something like that. We'll wait for the others, and if they don't have anything, I'll ride out to Edie's place."

"Si, señor. Perhaps she knows."

Jason said, "You will be in charge of the vaqueros. Put two or three lookouts around the place so that we won't be taken by surprise."

"Si." The man trotted away.

Jason made himself a smoke and stared into the darkness. There were lights in the house behind him and he felt pulled that way, yet he didn't move. He couldn't help thinking of the early years, of Edie when they were first married. They'd had several months together before the trouble started. Jason Mellor had not then been such a well-known name.

He couldn't blame her for leaving him. He had never blamed her, because he understood. He thought of what it must have been like for her afterward, in that Colorado mining town. An expression of pure fury crossed his face.

She could have quit, he told himself. Later, she could have changed. Perhaps she could change even now. But he knew it wasn't true. And even if she could change, the life she had led would always be a wall between them, a wall that could never come down.

He'd have to go out and see her tonight, unless one of the other trackers turned up with something. And he didn't want to go. He didn't want to be torn again, with anger at the way she lived, with need and the desire for her, with shame because part of the blame for what she was rested squarely on him.

But he'd have to go. And he'd have to make her tell him who the killer was. For her own safety, and because catching Robles' killer was very important to him.

An hour passed before the second tracker came in. He had lost his trail in the tracks of a cattle herd near Roth's ranch. The others came in shortly thereafter with similar stories of failure. Jason glanced once at the house, then mounted his horse and rode away, north toward Edie's place.

A strange premonition seemed to ride with him tonight. It was as though he knew he were going to die soon. His past life paraded itself before his eyes, and it seemed as though, like written words, it was punctuated regularly with killings, each like a period signifying the end of something.

The first. . . . He could remember the things he had thought as a boy, the things he had felt. His heroes had been the gunfighters, the marshals in the trail towns, the buffalo hunters, the army scouts. He bought his first gun, an old Navy .36 caliber Colt's, from a drunken Union soldier recently discharged, for three dollars. He bought powder and ball for it and spent several hours a day practicing with it.

He learned that he had a knack with guns, an uncanny co-ordination of eye and hand. If he stared directly at the spot he wished to hit, he hit it, no matter in what position he held the gun. A dangerous skill for a sixteen-year-old boy, who was quick as a cat, who could snatch the gun from its holster faster than anyone else in town.

There were benches in front of the town saloon. On summer evenings men would gather there, to smoke, to talk, to spin tall tales. And one night there was a stranger, powerful, heavy browed, bragging of the men he'd killed.

"Bet you ain't even as fast as young Jason there," one of the townsmen said. "Bet Jason can outdraw you, an' outshoot you, too."

It started with that, but it didn't end there. The townsmen kept taunting the stanger because they didn't like his arrogance. Jason was drawn into it against his will.

When it was over—when the stranger lay dead and bloody in the street—they told Jason it wasn't going to make any difference. It had been self-defense, they said. It would be forgotten soon.

But it wasn't forgotten. Jason's friends avoided him. He couldn't get anyone to dance with him at the Saturday night dances in the Odd Fellows Hall. Men looked at him as though he were something strange and dangerous. Even his father and mother changed toward him.

So he left. And the long, bitter cycle of death began.

He could have stopped at first, he supposed. He could have thrown away the gun. But he was angry, by then, at the injustice of all that had happened to him. He'd been drawn into that first gunfight against his will and because he was too young to avoid it.

The second . . . he remembered that one almost as clearly as the first. But from the third one on they began to fade in his memory. He remembered some of the faces vaguely, yet of late all the faces held resemblances to that of the last, to Burt Nordyke's. There had been eleven in all.

He'd met Edie in Wichita, after he'd already killed five men. He'd married her and he'd really tried to quit. He'd buried the gun in the bottom of a suitcase and had started out across the plains to stake a homestead claim. But by that time it was too late to quit. He was too well known, perhaps because he was so young to have killed so many men.

The miles passed swiftly beneath his horse's hoofs, unnoticed in his preoccupation with his thoughts. Suddenly he saw the light of Edie's house ahead of him.

Would she have visitors tonight? he wondered. And if she did, could he wait patiently for his turn to be with her? He shook his head almost violently. If she had visitors he'd make them leave.

But as he approached the house he saw no horses tied to the hitching post in the yard. He knocked loudly on the door.

There was the sound of steps, and a moment later the door opened. Her expression was smiling, but the smile was false and it faded the instant she saw who he was.

He had seen the smile she gave her customers, and

the fact that he had was embarrassing to them both. She said coldly, "What do you want?"

"I want to talk to you."

She stood aside. "I don't suppose I can stop you. Come in."

He went in and closed the door behind him. "Are you expecting anyone tonight?"

"Is that what you came to talk about?"

He shook his head. Her hostility was upsetting, but he supposed it would make this easier. He said, "I want to know who killed Sandoval Robles. You'll have to tell me who turned his horse loose here and took one of yours."

She shook her head in refusal.

He said, "I want to know as much for your safety as for anything else. If the killer is running loose, he's dangerous to you."

She smiled bitterly. "And if I tell you, do you think anyone would believe the word of a . . ." She seemed unable to say the word. "Do you think anyone is likely to believe *me*?"

"Why wouldn't they? Miguel trailed him here, and he, Jethro, Peligan and I will all back up what you say."

She shook her head stubbornly. "I won't tell you, Jason."

He asked, "How did you get this land and this house? It's right in the middle of Grandee."

She flushed darkly. Jason said, "Sandoval Robles gave it to you, didn't he?"

"The land. I got the house built with money I had saved."

"Don't you owe him anything for giving you the

land? Don't you owe it to him to tell me who his killer is?''

"I don't—he—" She became suddenly confused.

"He visited you, is that it?"

"What if he did? He was old, but he was good to me.''

Jason gripped her shoulders. He said harshly, ''Edie, this man, whoever he is, knows you are the only one who can tell his name. Do you think he's going to let you live? Do you think keeping still will keep you safe? He just hasn't gotten around to you, that's all. When he's had time to think, he will.''

Her face paled but she shook her head stubbornly.

Jason said, ''With Robles dead, they're going to be moving onto Grandee from all sides. I'm not going to have time to guard you, and I can't spare any men for it.''

"I don't need any guards. I can take care of myself.'' But her voice was not as positive as it might have been.

He shrugged. ''All right, Edie. I'll come by here to see you as often as I can. And if you should change your mind, you can come to Grandee and stay until the killer is caught.''

She nodded faintly. ''Thank you, Jason. But I will be all right.''

He wanted to shake her. She was so confident of her ability to handle men—But she'd never tried handling a killer before. However, he knew that there was nothing further he could do. He stared down at her, feeling the old pull in spite of the things he knew about her. He turned abruptly and went to the door.

She said softly, ''I'm sorry, Jason. I wish . . .''

He turned his head. ''What?''

"Nothing. Never mind. It's just too bad, that's all. About you and me. But we could never make it together now."

He stood frozen for an instant. She wanted to try again with him—or thought she did. It was there in her voice.

He wanted to turn from the door and go to her; he could not fully understand why he did not. He said softly, "No, I don't suppose we could." He opened the door and stepped outside, closed it behind him and stood for a moment on the stoop.

Pulled two ways. . . . With a soft curse, he crossed to his horse and swung astride.

She *was* in danger, whether she believed she was or not. Frowning, he rode out of the yard and headed toward Grandee. Something elusive troubled him, something he could not quite comprehend. There was a key in something she had said. He went back over their conversation in his mind, searching for it.

He was halfway to Grandee before he finally gave it up. Groping for it was like staring too hard into darkness, trying to see some shadow, some wraith. Perhaps if he stopped thinking about it for a while, it would come to him.

He wished he could spare a couple of men to guard her place, but he knew he could not. In the coming days he would need every man he had.

Lights were blazing from the main house at Grandee as he approached. There were lanterns in the courtyard, and lamps glowed from many of the adobe huts belonging to the vaqueros. Vaguely uneasy, Jason approached, holding his horse to a silent walk.

Chapter 12

Just at the edge of light streaming out of the courtyard, Jason halted his horse. He sat for a moment, wondering at all the activity. The hour was very late and everybody should have been in bed.

He heard a soft scuff nearby and swung his head warily. His gun was out of its holster and the hammer made a soft click as it came back.

A voice—Miguel's—murmured, "Señor. It is only I."

Jason said, "What's going on?"

"It is the sheriff, señor. He is here with a posse, asking for you. I think he means to take you prisoner."

Jason heard some soft scuffing noises and eight or ten shapes materialized out of the darkness. Miguel said, "We have been waiting for you to return, señor. We have our guns. If you do not wish to be the sheriff's prisoner . . . "

Jason said, "Bueno. I do not wish to be the sheriff's

prisoner. Let's go in and see if that's what he wants.''

Riding slowly, followed by the heavily armed vaqueros and Miguel, he entered the courtyard. Proust and four men were waiting in the center of it. Their horses stood with trailing reins nearby. Jason rode directly to the sheriff and stared down at him questioningly.

Proust glanced at Miguel and at the vaqueros behind him, who had fanned out slightly until they formed a semicircle around him and his men. He fumbled in the pocket of his coat and brought out two papers. He said, ''I have two warrants for your arrest.''

''Who swore them out?''

The sheriff opened one. ''This one was sworn out by Juan Robles. It charges you with the murder of Sandoval Robles.''

Jason frowned. ''I didn't expect you to be on my side, but I didn't expect anything like this, either. Do you serve a warrant for anyone that wants to swear one out? You know damned well I didn't kill Sandoval Robles. You followed the tracks from the place he was killed. You read sign at the scene.''

Proust shrugged noncommittally.

Jason asked, ''What's the other one?''

''It was sworn out by a man named Nordyke. He charges you with the murder of his brother.''

''And you're willing to throw me in jail on two fake warrants? You know what will happen if I let you do it, don't you? In twenty-four hours there won't be anything left of Grandee.'' He scowled. ''Have you thought about what will come afterward? You'll have more scrapping on your hands than you've had since you've been sheriff here.''

"I'll take that chance. Give me your gun and let's get started."

Jason laughed dryly. "Huh uh. I'm not going anyplace. Take those warrants and. . . . Well, just take 'em back with you and forget 'em."

"You're refusing to go with me?"

Jason nodded curtly.

Proust glanced at Miguel and the vaqueros, then at Jason again. He said, "I suppose you know that you're resisting arrest? And that I can charge every one of these men of yours with obstructing an officer in the performance of his duty?"

Jason turned his head, thoroughly disillusioned now. He said, "Hear that, Miguel?"

"Si, señor. We have heard. I think we are not very frightened."

Jason grinned coldly at Proust. "It's your move."

"You'll regret this." Proust's eyes were furious, but Jason detected something in them that made him believe the sheriff's anger was directed at himself as much as at Jason.

He interrupted, "You might be the one to do the regretting, if it turns out you picked the losing side."

"I do what I think. . . ."

Jason finished sourly, ". . . is right? If you can talk yourself into believing that, then you've got nothing to worry about."

Proust swung his head and spoke to one of his men. "Get the horses." He turned and stared up at Jason. "Better change your mind, Mellor. If you don't come with me now, you're an outlaw. The word will go out that you're to be taken dead or alive."

Jason said, "It's open season on me anyway."

Proust's man led the horses to him. He took the reins of his own and mounted heavily. His men followed suit. Proust glanced once at Jason, then turned and led them thundering out of the courtyard.

Miguel said softly, "The señora wished to speak with you when you returned."

Jason nodded. He dismounted, gave the reins to one of the vaqueros, and walked toward the house. He realized suddenly how tired he was. Sleep had been a luxury lately. And he had not yet fully recovered from the effects of his wound.

Before he could reach the door, it opened. He knew Clare had been watching as he talked with the sheriff and his men. He went in and she asked worriedly, "What did the sheriff want?"

"He had a couple of warrants for me. One was sworn out by Juan, charging me with the murder of his father. The other was sworn out by the man your husband saved me from when I first came here."

"And you refused to go with him?"

He nodded.

"Now . . ." There was terror in her eyes.

He shrugged. "It's open season on me anyway. And I didn't expect any support from Proust."

Her eyes searched his face. "You've got to go. You can't stay here. Take Miguel and enough vaqueros to make sure you get safely away. I couldn't stand it if . . ."

Jason looked down into her face. Having someone care whether he lived or died was a new experience for him. Her eyes were brimming with tears and her lips were trembling.

The reassuring words that were on lips were never

spoken, because he knew even before they came out that they weren't true. His chances of remaining alive if he stayed were extremely poor.

He said, "You know I can't go. There are too many things to hold me here. Your husband saved my life, and when he was dying he asked me to stay."

The tears spilled across her cheeks.

He said, "And there's you. I don't think I want to live if I can't have you."

She was suddenly sobbing uncontrollably. He put out his arms and she ran into them. Her body, warm and soft, shook with her weeping. Her hair was smooth and fragrant against his face.

He said softly, "This will not last long. In a week it will be over. They will have made their try at taking what they want of Grandee, and they'll have given up."

"A week." She turned her face up toward his. "A week . . ." He knew she was measuring the living that remained to him. His arms tightened.

With her face buried against his chest she whispered, "Jason, I want you to know about my husband and myself. I want you to know just how it was."

"You don't need . . ."

"I want to, Jason. It's important to me that you know."

He said, "All right."

"My father and Sandoval Robles were good friends. My father was foreman here long before I was born. When he died—well, Sandoval Robles had promised him part of Grandee. He wanted to give it to me but he knew that people would talk about it. He knew it would ruin my reputation. So he suggested we be married so that I would get it when he died. It was a marriage of convenience, Jason, and we were never husband and wife. But we liked and respected each other.''

He had supposed it was something like this, although he had never really understood before. He was glad she had told him. It removed the last doubt about staying . . . removed the guilt he had felt over his attraction to her while Sandoval Robles was still alive.

She murmured, ''But you've got to go. When it's all over, I'll come wherever you are.''

He shook his head. ''Do you know what I am, what I've been? I've been like a wild animal, always on the move from town to town. Every place I go I'm recognized. There's always some kid who has to challenge me. That's no life for you. The same thing would happen to us that happened to Edie and me.''

''No, I . . .''

He put a hand gently over her mouth. ''Wait. Listen. Your husband offered me a chance to change all that. He told me that on Grandee there was no such thing as a personal challenge. He said that when someone challenged a man of Grandee he challenged all of Grandee. Don't you see, it's my chance to forget I ever owned a gun? It's my chance to live like other men, to put down roots.''

She looked up at him. ''But if you're . . .''

''. . . . killed? If I leave I may be killed in the first town I reach. Over nothing. Because some kid wonders whether he's as fast as I am. Here, at least, I'll be trying to do something worthwhile.''

She nodded reluctantly. ''All right, Jason. But be careful, please. Be careful. I couldn't stand to lose you now.''

He bent his head and kissed her on the mouth. Her response was almost desperate.

Jason pulled away with a mild curse as he heard Miguel calling from outside the house, "Señor?"

He opened the door and stepped outside. Clare stood framed in the doorway behind him. Miguel said, "Horsemen approach. Five—six—I cannot tell."

Jason listened. He heard the pound of approaching hoofs. It drew closer until it seemed the horsemen were about to enter the courtyard. A volley of shots racketed and the sound of hoofbeats began to diminish. Jason crossed the courtyard. A vaquero ran to him, leading a horse. He swung astride.

Miguel shouted in Spanish, "Is anybody hurt?"

He was answered by a dozen voices in the negative. Jason said, "Take three or four men and follow them. This may be a feint to draw us away."

Miguel thundered out of the courtyard with four men following him. After several moments the sound of their horse's hoofs was only a dull rumble, rapidly fading away.

Jason mounted and rode out, frowning thoughtfully. He rode a circle around the house, then widened the circle to include all the headquarters buildings. He saw nothing, heard nothing, There seemed to be no reason. . . .

He headed back. And as he did, he saw a group of horsemen ahead, moving to intercept him. Miguel, he thought. Then, against the lights, he caught a silhouette . . . another.

Suddenly he understood the flurry of shots fired in the hit-and-run attack. They hadn't been meant to hit anything. They had been intended to draw the vaqueros away from him, or him away from the house. The men cutting him off from the Grandee buildings were Sheriff Proust and his possemen.

Jason yelled, "Proust, go home. Unless you want to take some dead men home with you!"

He heard Proust's voice. "Get him!"

A rifle boomed, its sound echoing back from the buildings ahead. A flurry of pistol shots followed. Jason's horse leaped ahead, reared, and fell.

He was out of the saddle before the horse came back on him, barely avoiding the flailing hoofs. His gun was in his hand, but he was afoot. Again the rifle boomed, and again. The pistol shots were continuous, like an irregularly exploding string of firecrackers. Shapes moved toward him, fanning out, encircling.

They meant to kill him, he thought. There had been no demand that he surrender himself. There would be no such demand.

Crouching, he ran directly toward the house. He fired as a horseman loomed on his right, and heard the bullet strike the horse. The man yelled wildly as he fell.

They were converging on him now. Suddenly he stopped, put an arm up across his mouth to muffle his voice and yelled exultantly. "I got the son-of-a-bitch, Proust! I got him!"

They thundered to the downed horse, four of them. They swung from their horses, running as they hit the ground, and converged on the man that was down.

Approaching silently, Jason seized the reins of one of their mounts. He swung to the saddle and dug heels into the horse's sides. He bent low in the saddle as he thundered toward the house.

Their yells were furious. Shots racketed behind him. Jason heard one bullet go by so close it sounded like an angry bee. He was clear, and untouched. But he couldn't help wondering what kind of pressure, what kind of bribe had been offered Proust to make him try a stunt like this.

Juan Robles, Roth, Nordyke . . . all three wanted Jason dead more than they wanted anything else. He had an eerie feeling that, with three of them after him so determinedly, he probably wouldn't live through the week.

Chapter 13

Just beyond the edge of the clustered buildings, Miguel and his vaqueros met Jason. One of them dismounted and gave up his horse. Jason released the horse he had been riding, mounted the other and rode back toward the house. The vaquero who had given him his horse climbed up behind one of the others.

When he could breathe normally again, Jason said, "That was Proust. I think he's gone back to town for tonight, but we'll see him again."

Miguel breathed. "The son-of-a-beetch!"

Jason grinned at him. "Si. That's exactly how I feel."

They rode into the courtyard. Immediately Jason saw the lathered horse and the excited vaquero waiting for him. The man said breathlessly, "Señor! To the east! I have come upon a camp just inside the border of Grandee. I have counted nine men moving around the fire."

"Who are they?"

"Juan Robles is there. So in Señor Sheets. And Delehanty and Moore and Brown. There are four strangers, but I heard a name spoken. It was. . . ." The man hesitated. "Norton?"

Jason said, "Nordyke?"

"That was it, Señor. Nordyke."

Jason turned his head. "Miguel, get the men ready. We'll ride in an hour. Have them eat and get provisions for a couple of days. Have them each take fifty rounds."

"Si, señor."

Jason himself felt near to exhaustion. He stumbled along the gallery to his room, went inside and collapsed upon the bed. He closed his eyes. . . .

He was sure he could not have slept more than five minutes. But when Miguel, shaking him, spoke, he knew it must have been closer to an hour. "Señor, it is time to go. And another of our vaqueros has just come in."

Jason got to his feet and staggered as he headed for the door. He went out into the gallery, rubbing his eyes, but refreshed for all his grogginess.

The vaquero was waiting outside his room. "Señor, I rode to the west of here. I thought it would be well to look at Señor Roth's ranch, so I did. He has a herd, señor, of what seemed to be nearly five hundred head. He has corraled the cattle and waits only for dawn to drive them onto Grandee."

Jason asked, "How many men?"

"Eleven saddles are hanging on the corral, señor. The men were inside the house."

Jason nodded. Elena came shuffling along the gallery. "Señor, there is food."

He nodded. He hated to take time to eat, but knew he should. Besides, he needed time to think. He had to decide which of the two forces he would hit. He couldn't go after both because he didn't have enough men for it.

He followed Elena along the gallery and into the house. Clare was waiting in the kitchen. He sat down at the table and she filled his plate, watching his face closely. He rubbed his unshaven chin ruefully, then grinned up at her.

"I've never been able to understand how a woman could stand a man when he looked like this."

Her answering smile was forced, and worry remained in her eyes. She said, "It isn't difficult."

He ate quickly, hungrily, weighing, as he did so, the problem of deciding which force he should attack. Miguel came to the door. "Señor, there is something Rodriguez forgot to tell you."

Jason waited. Miguel said, "It is that Juan Robles was getting ready to leave Señor Sheets' camp. Perhaps they have disagreed."

Jason frowned. "Maybe."

Clare said, "Maybe they *have* quarreled, Jason. Maybe. . . ."

He nodded. He would like to believe that a quarrel had split Juan away from Sheets. But he doubted if it would have come this soon. Later, perhaps, if they suceeded, the pair would quarrel over division of the spoils. But not just yet.

One force in the east, one in the west. They would

cut Grandee squarely in two. Once they had done that, others, the neighbors of Grandee to north and south, would move in too. And the whole thing would have a certain questionable legality, since Juan owned half of Grandee—or would—once the estate had been settled by the courts.

Jason's only chance was to win overwhelmingly. Proust had said he was an outlaw, to be taken dead or alive. But if he won. . . . Grandee was still a force to be reckoned with, by Proust and by the courts. If he won and managed to keep Grandee intact. . . .

Juan's departure from Sheets' camp continued to bother Jason. If you ruled out a quarrel, he thought, there was only one other explanation for it. Juan had something to do that only he *could* do.

Suddenly Jason cursed softly under his breath. If Juan Robles was the murderer, that might explain many things. It would explain why Edie had said no one would believe her even if she named the murderer. She had doubted if anyone would take the word of a prostitute against that of Juan Robles. And if they didn't her life wouldn't be worth much after she told her story.

Juan's leaving Sheets' camp in the middle of the night—perhaps he was uneasy, Jason thought, knowing that Edie knew. He might be heading for her place right now, to close her mouth for good.

Jason felt an almost frantic uncertainty. If he were going to save Edie's life. . . . But he didn't dare go there himself. Miguel and the vaqueros could handle neither invading force by themselves. Besides, he didn't know for sure that Juan *was* headed for Edie's place. It was all guesswork, and he could easily be wrong.

He got up nervously, paced to the door and back. Sheets, Delehanty, Moore and Brown were all gunmen. They composed the toughest group. They would inflict the most serious losses upon Jason and his men. It therefore seemed sensible to attack Roth's group first. Edie would have to wait.

He went to the door and stepped out onto the gallery. He said, "Miguel, send Rodriguez to Edie's place. Juan may have gone there. If he did, he'll try to kill her. Tell Rodriguez to stop him, any way he can. And call Jethro and Peligan."

"Si, señor." Miguel moved away silently in the darkness.

Jason turned to Clare. "We can't possibly get back before late afternoon or evening. Don't look for us until then."

She came to him and put both hands up to his face. Gently she drew his head down until she could kiss him on the mouth. She made a face, but her eyes were shining with tears.

"Whiskers! When are you going to shave them off?"

He grinned. "Manana." He turned, strode across to the horse the vaqueros had saddled for him, and swung to the saddle. Jethro and Peligan came across the courtyard and mounted the horses that had been saddled for them. Jason led out, heading west. Miguel spurred alongside him.

Jason knew there was only one way he could win today. He would have to be merciless. He would have

to hit them hard and hurt them so badly in the first
assault that they'd have no heart for further fight.

Riding, he kept watching the eastern horizon behind
him, looking for signs of coming dawn. He hoped he
could get there before Roth had reason to expect him.

He counted the men with him. Besides Miguel,
Jethro, and Peligan, there were six. Ten, then, against
eleven, the number of saddles the vaquero had counted
hanging on Roth's corral. But on the side of Grandee
would be the element of surprise. And Roth's men
would be scattered, preoccupied with driving their herd
onto Grandee grass.

The miles flowed steadily behind. Jason set a pace
which would spare their horses as much as possible.
They had to return to Grandee before they could get
fresh mounts. Gradually the horizon behind them
turned a faint, dark gray. The light grew steadily until
gray had spread across the entire sky.

Jason found himself thinking almost constantly of
Edie, worrying about her. A dozen times he hesitated
on the point of halting the men and changing course.
But he never did.

If she'd only told him last night. . . . He could have
taken her to Grandee. He could have hidden her out
someplace, in some vaquero's adobe house. She would
have been safe right now.

Perhaps, returning from the fight with Roth, he could
detour enough to go by Edie's place. But the thought
brought no relief from worry. His mind did not stop
imagining Juan Robles—who, it now appeared, might
have shot his own father from behind—with her,
perhaps even now killing her.

He spurred his horse savagely and let it run. The sky

turned pink, then gradually blue. The sun poked its golden rim above the plain. Jason watched closely for dust hanging in the air ahead. Five hundred cattle would stir up quite a lot of dust. It should be easily visible. And once they'd spotted it, they could make their plans for reaching the drovers unobserved.

The land was rolling here. Its inequalities were almost like ocean swells, gentle hills and wide valleys sometimes cut at the bottom with a dry wash.

Fifty miles away, snow-covered peaks were barely visible in the clear morning air. A few thin, horizontal clouds hung like wisps above the peaks. The grass on Grandee was thick and tall. It brushed Jason's feet as he rode. They left a wide, plainly visible trail as they rode through it. This was a day, he thought, when the minds of men should be occupied with other things than greed and violence.

He wondered briefly how it all would end. He wanted to stay here, and he wanted Clare more than he had ever wanted anything else. He would be glad to hang up his gun and try to forget the men who had fallen before it.

It would be good work, to have each day dawn exactly like the last. It would be good to be weary, and hungry, and to rest and eat. It would be good to have friends, and roots, perhaps even sons.

The sun came up and beat hotly against his back. At last he picked up what appeared to be a column of dust, faint with distance, ahead and to his left. He pointed it out to Miguel. The man's dark face lighted with anticipation.

Peligan said, "It's them, all right. How are you going to work this out?"

Jason shrugged. "We'll have to take a look at how the land lies, when we get close to them. They'll be scattered out, driving their herd. We'll try and hit 'em before they can bunch up. And we'll hit them hard. Kill their horses first and put 'em afoot. If they don't give up then . . ."

Peligan nodded matter-of-factly.

Jason said, "And when they're beat, we'll stampede their herd back in the direction they came."

He stayed, now, in the wide valleys, always keeping a ridge between himself and the dust he had sighted earlier. Occasionally he would ride far enough up the side of a ridge to take a brief look over the top.

Steadily they closed the distance between themselves and the herd. At last, when Jason judged they were close enough, he had them dismount and work their way carefully to a ridge from which they could all look directly down at the slow-traveling herd.

Jethro said, "It's Roth, all right. I'd know that bastard anywhere."

Jason nodded. He frowned as he studied the land that lay directly ahead of the traveling herd. They were in a wide valley that continued unbroken for a considerable distance. But about three miles ahead the valley forked, joined another and then continued.

It was a perfect place for an ambush. Jason could reach the fork with his men without being seen, attack from the front and turn the cattle back. He could send some of his men over the low ridge to attack from behind.

He pointed the fork out to Miguel, Jethro and Peligan, but he spoke Spanish for the vaqueros' benefit. When he had explained his plan of action and was sure everyone understood, he eased himself back from the ridge until he was far enough below its crest to stand up. The others followed suit.

Mounting, he cautioned, "Remember, kill the horses first. Put the men afoot. And stampede the cattle."

"Si, señor. Si." There was excitement in the vaqueros and in Miguel, but to Jethro and Peligan this was just another job like many they had done in the past.

Given time, Jason thought, he would be like them. Inevitably he would tire of always being hunted like a wolf. He'd take a job for some big rancher who wanted him only for his gun. And he'd kill for pay.

Then his thoughts asked bluntly if that wasn't exactly what he was doing now. He shook his head almost imperceptibly. He was fighting for many things, but money wasn't one of them. He was fighting for a place, a home, a life where he wouldn't have to kill again. He was fighting for a woman he needed and wanted desperately. He was fighting for a dead man who had saved his life and offered him a chance to change the course of it.

Chapter 14

Down country he led his men, trotting his horse sometimes, or lifting it occasionally to a slow, rocking lope, but watching, always that no large amount of dust came from the horses' hoofs. It wouldn't do to be spotted now. He had a notion that after the other day, when he'd had fifteen of Roth's cattle killed, the man would be as savage as Jason himself intended to be.

The tight, empty feeling in his stomach, the one he'd experienced so often before, came to him now and he realized with a start that for the first time in his life he was entering a battle in the company of other men. Always before he had been alone.

Strangely enough, he did not find their company reassuring. He was used to fighting alone, to worrying only about himself. Now he had to worry about all of them.

He knew exactly how he planned it, but he wasn't sure it would go that way. Each party, the one attacking from the front and the one attacking from the rear, would center their attention upon the drovers nearest them. Unthinkingly, Roth's men would rush to their aid singly, instead of grouping and then coming on. If it went that way, all would be well. Roth's men would be defeated and scattered, probably without inflicting any considerable damage upon the forces of Grandee.

But if, on the other hand, Roth grouped his men immediately after the initial attack—then it could turn into quite a fight. It could even result in defeat for Grandee. Confusion, then, as well as surprise, would have to be one of Jason's weapons.

He turned his head. "Jethro, you and Peligan take three of the vaqueros and hit them from the rear. Miguel and I will take the others and hit them from the front." He waited a moment and then added, "Do a lot of yelling and shooting. Ride in fast. We don't want them to know they outnumber us."

The vaqueros were grinning, their dark eyes bright. Miguel was as impassive as an Indian. Jethro and Peligan seemed matter-of-fact.

They reached the low point of the ridge that separated the forking valleys. Jason dismounted and walked carefully around it, then ducked suddenly and trotted back to his horse. He said, "Point man is less than a quarter mile away. Jethro, you and Peligan get going."

"Okay. Come one, three of you." Three of the vaqueros joined the pair and the five rode angling up the ridge in the direction from which they had come.

Jason called, "When you hear the first shot, move in."

He mounted, grinned at Miguel and the vaqueros.

"Remember, I want lots of noise. I want 'em to think we've got twenty men."

"Si, señor. Si!"

Jason said, "All right, let's go!" As he spoke, he dug spurs into his horse's sides and the animal leaped ahead.

He was around the point almost immediately and heading straight toward the man riding point. He swung his head and gestured at his men to fan out. Drawing his revolver, he fired twice into the air.

Glancing up and to his right, he saw Jethro, Peligan and those with them come galloping over the crest of the ridge. He saw the white, startled, dusty face of the man riding point, then glimpsed the bulky figure of Roth on the flank closest to Jethro's force.

Roth hadn't seen them yet. He spurred his horse toward Jason and turned his head to yell at the men behind him. Jason was now less than a hundred yards from the man riding point. He grinned to himself, knowing that Roth's words couldn't carry over the noise of the bawling, slow-traveling herd.

It was fortunate that Roth had been caught on that particular flank. He'd be one of the first to go down. He wouldn't be able to rally his men.

Behind Jason, Miguel and the vaqueros were howling like madmen and shooting their guns into the air. The man riding point turned to flee.

Jason fired, from a range of nearly fifty yards. His bullet hit the hindquarters of the rider's horse. The animal went down, then got up and tried to run, dragging one hind leg. Jason fired again. This time the horse fell and did not get up. The man was rolling in the deep, dry grass. He had a rifle in his hands.

Jason was nearly on top of him. He stared at the gaping barrel of the gun. . . . He fired a third time instinctively. Then his gun clicked emptily.

From a corner of his eye Jason caught a blur of movement, a glimpse of red. Miguel had launched himself from his horse directly at the man on the ground. The red was his headband worn Apache style around his head.

The rifle roared and black smoke billowed from its muzzle. Then Miguel's body struck that of the man on the ground, and the sun glinted briefly on the blade of a knife. . . . Miguel stood up, wiping the blade on his pants. There was a spot of blood that had not come from the knife on his left upper sleeve.

Jason yelled, "You're hit!"

Miguel flashed him a grin, "*Es nada, señor*," He sheathed the knife and leaped to the back of his horse.

Jason stared into the rising cloud of dust. The cattle had turned from the howling, shooting men riding toward them. Those on the flank had turned from Jethro's men into the herd itself. But those on the right and in the rear had not yet started to move. The result was a close-packed, milling herd that neither Roth's men nor Jason's could get through.

Jason reloaded hastily, riding at top speed toward the place where he had last seen Roth. The dust swirled aside long enough for him to see Jethro and Peligan leading their men toward the rear of the herd.

It closed down again, and out of its billowing obscurity galloped a rider. It was Roth, his face streaked with blood and dust. His eyes were wild with fury. His horse collided with Miguel's and knocked Miguel's animal to its knees. Roth's horse plunged on.

Jason whirled his own startled mount. The animal reared with excitment, then came down and surged into a run. Jason knew where Roth was headed. He was trying to reach the far side of the herd so he could assemble his men.

Jason could hear the beat of hoofs behind him and turned his head. He couldn't see either Miguel or the vaqueros, but he knew they were following.

At times the figure of Roth's horse, ahead, would disappear into the swirling dust. At times it would reappear. Roth was riding crouched low over the horse's withers. He did not look back. The herd remained an imponderable. In minutes now the cattle would stampede. But in which direction? Jason couldn't guess.

Whoever was caught in the path of the herd. . . . Five hundred cattle would knock a horse and rider down. They might only detour the horse, but they would pound the man into an unrecognizable mass of flesh and blood.

Roth reached the far side of the herd. His yells drifted back to Jason's ears as he shouted to his men and tried to rally them. An ominous rumble came from the milling cattle. In seconds now they would begin to move, picking up speed as they thinned out, rolling over everything in their path.

Jason raked his horse savagely with his spurs. The animal gave him a burst of even greater speed. He began slowly, to gain on Roth. Over the noise of the rumbling herd, he caught the sound of a burst of gunshots ahead. Jethro and Peligan, he thought, jumping Roth's men in the drag of the herd.

Roth thundered past his swing rider on this side and

yelled at him frantically, his voice holding more than anger now. Jason heard fear in it, too. The man was slow to move, and by the time he had spurred his horse and turned, Jason was alongside him.

The rider's face was white, his teeth bared in a grimace of surprise. Jason raised his gun. The man tried to bring his rifle to bear. Jason fired once and the rider's horse pitched forward, throwing the man clear.

Half a dozen steers crossed Jason's path, between him and the fleeing Roth. Their eyes rolled at him in sheer terror. The stampede was coming this way, then. There was another sudden burst of shots ahead, somewhat closer now. More cattle streamed past in front of Jason's horse. Suddenly the mount veered so suddenly it almost unseated him. He felt a steer's sharp horn rake his leg.

He was in the midst of them; then his horse running free with them. Jason kept trying to pull right, trying to see into the pall of dust. Roth must have turned too, he thought.

This hadn't gone as he had planned at all. He and Miguel and four vaqueros were caught in the stampede. They'd be scattered. Several miles might be traveled before they could ease themselves to the edge of the herd and out of it. Some of them might go down and be trampled.

And behind . . . Jethro and Peligan and their three vaqueros were outnumbered, unless they had managed to even the odds before the stampede began. Jason reloaded his gun with difficulty. He shot the steer crowding him from the right, and the animal went down. Jason pulled his horse over into the space the steer's falling made.

He shot another steer, and another, pulling right each time. He reloaded again and shot two more steers in rapid succession. His legs were bleeding from horn gouges. His horse's sides were bleeding, too. Dust filled Jason's nostrils and sound filled his ears.

Up over a ridge they went, and down into the shallow valley below. Suddenly Jason caught a glimpse of Roth. The man was thirty or forty yards ahead and slightly to his right.

Jason yelled, "Roth!" but his voice was lost in the steady roar.

He spurred his horse, but the animal, hemmed in on all four sides, could go no faster. Gradually, as they ran themselves out, the cattle began to spread and thin. Jason was able to gain slightly on Roth. The two reached the edge of the herd at the same time. Roth pulled his plunging horse to a halt.

Jason followed suit. Roth turned, and the two were suddenly face to face across an open space of fifty feet. It was an instant before recognition touched Roth's heavy features. Jason supposed his own face was as caked with dust as Roth's. He licked his lips and felt grit between his teeth.

He had never seen a more furious face in his life than Roth's. He knew he was going to have to kill the man or be killed himself. Roth raised the gun he was holding in his hand. His horse danced nervously.

Jason's own gun lined itself on the man's deep chest. He wondered how many unspent cartridges were left in it. He'd reloaded and shot four times . . . or was it five? One shot at most, then. One was all he could possibly have left in the gun.

Roth fired. Jason felt something like a burn sear

across the thick muscles of his thigh. For an instant the pain was excruciating. It was as if someone had laid a red-hot iron against his thigh.

Tired as he was, worried as he was, the pain suddenly made him furious. He fired, and saw Roth's body jerk with the bullet's impact. But Roth wasn't seriously hurt. He spurred his horse and came thundering straight toward Jason.

Jason fired again and heard the hammer's empty click. Then Roth's horse struck his own and both animals and riders went down into a kicking, squealing, shouting heap.

Trying to get clear, Jason was struck in the forehead by a flailing hoof. He was flung away, his head reeling, his vision blurring. He saw Roth come crawling toward him.

He shook his head and struggled to his feet. Roth's shoulder struck him in the belly and drove a monstrous grunt of air from him. Nausea choked him. The pair rolled in the dusty grass, kneeing, gouging, each fully aware that this was a battle to the death.

Roth's gun was in his hand. It must be empty, Jason thought groggily, or Roth would have used it again. The man kept trying to strike a killing blow with its barrel, and Jason kept trying to avoid it until his senses came back to him.

Roth's knee struck Jason's wounded thigh. With the sudden rush of pain, Jason's senses returned to him briefly, sharp and clear. He put both hands on Roth's gun arm and twisted viciously. The gun dropped and Roth yelled. Jason released his arm and seized his throat. He began to beat Roth's head methodically against the ground.

Loss of blood from the leg wound, and weariness, were beginning to weaken him. But suddenly Roth's body went limp. Jason stumbled to his feet. He stared down at Roth, at the man's chest, which was still rising and fally regularly. He hated to leave Roth here alive. But he knew he couldn't kill the man—not when Roth was lying unconscious on the ground.

He stumbled to his horse, drew his gun from its holster, and began to eject the empties and reload the gun from his cartridge belt. He shoved the reloaded gun back into its holster, then stared at his thigh, at his blood-soaked pants leg.

Several riders pounded toward him and rode on past, following the pall of dust left in the wake of the stampeding herd. They went by with only the briefest glance at him.

He climbed to the back of his horse and turned in the direction he had come. The forces of Grandee had won this battle, at least. Now he had to find out what the price of victory had been.

Chapter 15

Miguel was the first rider he saw. Miguel approached him from his right, angling along an intercepting course. His red headband was gone. It was tied around his upper arm. His eyes, as he approached, were on Jason's bloody thigh. He reached Jason and pulled up alongside.

"You are losing much blood, señor. Stop a moment and I will tie something around your leg.

Jason nodded. He hated to waste the time, but he feared his increasing weakness. Neither man dismounted. Miguel cut the pants leg expertly away from the wound. Jason pulled out his shirt and ripped it up the front. He tore off a strip reaching from tail to collar, about six inches wide, and gave it to Miguel.

Miguel tied it around the wound. By the time he had finished, Jason saw Jethro, Peligan and five vaqueros approaching them. Blood streaming from Peligan's ear and running down the side of his neck. One of the vaqueros held his left arm awkwardly and Jason knew, from the pain in his face, that it was broken. The others were dusty but apparently unhurt.

Jason's eyes were questioning. Jethro said, "We lost two, Jason. One in the stampede. The other was shot in the chest."

Jason nodded. He said, "Someone build a fire. We'll eat and have coffee, and then we'll go on."

He slid from his horse and stretched out wearily on the ground. The peculiarly pungent smell of burning buffalo chips filled his nostrils. After a while he smelled bacon frying and shortly afterward there was the odor of coffee. One of the vaqueros brought him a tin cup of it and a chunk of bread with a thick piece of bacon on top of it.

Jason sipped the coffee, fighting nausea. He drank about half of it and then began, determinedly, to eat the bacon and the bread. He got it all down, then gulped the coffee, trying to keep it down.

It stayed, but it was like a threatening lump in his stomach. The vaqueros put out the fire and mounted. Jason crawled into his own saddle with difficulty.

He hesitated only briefly about the direction he would take. Then he lined his horse out toward Edie's place. There would be clean bandages there, and water for washing wounds. And whisky to pour over them so they would not grow feverish. Besides, he was worried about her. His worry had lain, all through the fight, in the back of his mind.

He dozed sometimes as he rode at the head of the subdued and silent group. He needed rest, and so did the others. But there wasn't going to be time for rest. They'd pause briefly at Edie's place and then go on.

Occasionally he would rouse himself and glance behind at the men. The vaquero with the broken arm had it splinted now. Another of the men led two horses with the bodies of the dead tied across their saddles.

Jason doubted if Roth would try invading Grandee again. Two such stinging defeats would probably be enough for him. But there was still the other force to meet—with men who were exhausted and hurt. With fewer men than he had had before.

It was already well past noon. The sun was high and hot in the sky. The rolling, grassy miles gradually fell behind. In early afternoon, Jason sighted Edie's house ahead of him.

Half a mile from the place, he stopped, and studied it. There were several horses in the corral, but none were tied at Edie's door. A few white chickens scratched in the dusty yard.

It was peaceful looking. It seemed to drowse in the afternoon sun. And yet there was something about its appearance, or something within Jason himself. . . .

He said, "Fan out. Surround the place. If anybody tries to leave, take him. If you can't take him, shoot him."

Jethro and Peligan looked at him, puzzled. Miguel translated Jason's orders into Spanish for the vaqueros. Jason rode alone toward the house.

Something was wrong. The feeling increased steadily as he approached. And his mind kept remembering Edie, not as he had seen her last, but as she once had been. Young, fresh, as brightly shining as a newly minted coin. The shine had begun to tarnish almost from the day they were married, he thought ruefully.

Would he corrode Clare in the same way? Would his

past catch up with him in spite of Grandee, in spite of
Sandoval Robles' promises? He shook his head impatiently. He was now less than a hundred yards from
the house.

His leg throbbed steadily. It was bleeding yet, but the
thin bandage had helped to staunch the flow. At the
back door, he swung down from his horse, studying
the ground. There were fresh tracks here, overlaying all
the others. The tracks of a horse plunging to a stop
before the door. The tracks of a horse leaving, being
spurred mercilessly. There was a pile of droppings less
than an hour old.

Jason tied his horse and knocked. He heard nothing,
so he opened the door and went inside. Rodriguez lay in
the middle of the floor, his eyes open but with the
emptiness of death in them. Jason glanced at the door
leading to the rest of the house.

A sudden reluctance to continue touched him. But it
was more than reluctance, he realized. It was dread, as
though he knew what he was going to find. Suddenly,
impatiently, he crossed the kitchen and went through
the door.

She lay in the middle of the parlor floor, on a round
rag rug. She was on her side, facing the kitchen door,
and her eyes were open, staring at him with naked fear.

When she saw who he was the fear left her. Her lips
moved and sound came forth, but it was only a cry of
pain and relief, and had no words.

He hurried to her and knelt at her side. He said,
"How bad is it, Edie? What can I do?"

She smiled weakly. "It's bad. I should have told
you."

"Who was it?"

"Juan Robles. I knew my word wouldn't stand up against his. That's why I didn't tell you." Her voice faded. She made a grimace of pain and turned very pale. Beads of perspiration stood out on her forehead.

Jason didn't know what to say. He wanted to lift her, to help her, but he didn't want to hurt her more.

She whispered, "I got my house, my white house that I wanted so much. But it wasn't what I really wanted, Jason. I guess I wanted the things that go with white houses, and not the house at all."

He nodded. "I couldn't have given them to you, Edie. I'm sorry. I'm sorry you didn't meet someone else before you met me. Someone who could have. . . ."

Her hand came out and took his. She squeezed faintly. Her voice was weaker when it came. "Nobody gets just what they want, Jason. A person makes do with what they have. That's what I never learned. Until now. And now it's too late."

"No."

"Yes, Jason. But thank you for saying it isn't. It will help when. . . ."

He said, "Damn it, where are you hit? Maybe I can do something."

She didn't seem to hear his words. She said, "He came galloping to the house. He stormed inside without even bothering to knock. I heard the shot in the kitchen and then he came in here. He roared at me, 'Who have you told?' and when I shook my head and said, 'No one,' he yanked out his gun and shot. I guess he thought he had killed me, because when I came to he was gone. But I'm bleeding, Jason. I'm bleeding bad. I'm afraid."

Jason repeated, "Where?" Gently he moved her body until she was lying on her back. She smiled. "That's better. It doesn't hurt so much now."

Something was burning behind his eyes, and his throat felt tight. The front of her blouse was soaked with blood, and there was a stain of it on the rug underneath where she had been lying, but he couldn't move her. If he lifted her she'd probably die immediately.

She murmured in a voice he could scarcely hear, "Jason, I hope you do better than I did. I hope you find. . . ."

He could feel tears scalding his eyes and spilling across his cheeks. If only . . . . But it was too late for Edie. Too late. She closed her eyes. The faint smile on her lips faded. Her chest was still.

Jason stared at her face for a long, long time. Then he lifted her body, carried it to her bedroom and laid it gently on the bed. He walked to the window and stared outside.

His mind was filled with confusion. Gradually that faded and anger began to grow. He returned to the bed and stared down at Edie's face a moment more. It was peaceful now, relaxed and somehow younger looking than it had been in life. It was almost as though death had erased the marks that life had made on it.

He turned and strode through the door, crossed the parlor and went out through the kitchen. He mounted his horse and rode back to Miguel, Peligan, Jethro and the vaqueros.

He said, "She's dead. Juan killed her to keep her from telling anyone that he killed his father."

Miguel said, "I am sorry, señor."

Jason nodded. "Come on. We need bandages and we need food. We'll stop here for an hour and then we'll go on."

He led them into Edie's house. They trooped into the kitchen, silent and subdued in the presence of death. One of the vaqueros built up the fire and began to cook a meal. Others brought in water and put it on the stove to heat. Miguel found a clean sheet and ripped it into strips for bandaging.

Jason sat down, washed the ragged leg wound with water, then poured whisky over it. He sank back afterward, his head reeling, near unconsciousness, waiting for the pain to pass. When he could sit up again, he wound bandaging around the leg and tied the bandages. He took a long drink from the whisky bottle.

Miguel resplinted the vaquero's broken arm. Peligan bandaged his torn and bleeding ear by winding strips of cloth around his head. When he felt he could stand, Jason got up, crossed to Miguel, and washed and bandaged the flesh wound in Miguel's upper arm.

Two dead. Four wounded. Three of the wounded could fight, but the man with the broken arm was useless as a fighter now. Jason said, "Luis, stay here. I will need a wagon for the bodies just as soon as we get back to Grandee. If one doesn't come by this time tomorrow, bury her. Some place where there's shade. And some place where you can see the house. Bury Rodriguez, too."

He stopped suddenly, strode out the door, and walked across the yard.

Behind him at the house he could hear the sounds the

men made as they ate the meal that had been prepared. He wasn't hungry himself. He didn't want anything to eat—all he wanted now was to get his hands on Juan.

Somehow, some way, he had to defeat the force that Juan was with. In spite of being outnumbered. In spite of being forced to fight with men who were near exhaustion, not fresh as their opponents would be.

The men began trooping out of the house. They mounted and milled around, waiting. Jason crossed to his horse stiffly, limping on his wounded leg. He mounted awkwardly, because of both the pain and the stiffness of the bandaging.

He led out at a steady trot, heading south and slightly east. It was possible that Juan and Sheets had already reached Grandee headquarters and taken over. He wouldn't know until he reached a point directly east of the house. Then he would either find their trail or he would not.

Chapter 16

Nordyke, Sheets, Juan Robles—all three had reason to hate Jason bitterly. If they had already reached headquarters and taken it, then Jason was finished. He wouldn't have a chance. Even if they hadn't, his chances were poor enough.

He had not planned on the battle with Roth taking so much time. He shrugged lightly. Whatever happened, whatever he had to face, he supposed he'd have to accept it and go on from there.

The sun dropped slowly, inexorably, toward the horizon. The shadows lengthened and the air began to cool. When he was almost directly east of the house, with only a dozen miles to go, he sent Miguel galloping to Grandee headquarters to see if any more vaqueros had come in. He cautioned Miguel to approach it carefully. And now he began to watch the ground, looking for the invaders' trail.

His thoughts wandered. Edie had refused to name

Juan Robles as his father's murderer because she felt she would not be believed. But would Jason's word be any better than hers? If Juan and Sheets had taken Grandee headquarters, could Jason go to the sheriff and expect him to take the necessary action? He shook his head. There would be no legal recourse against Juan. Jason would have to handle it himself.

He reached a point directly east of Grandee without cutting any trails. He rode on for a couple of miles, on the chance that they might have swung slightly south. Still he found no trails. Encouraged, he turned back.

The sun was a golden ball just above the horizon when he sighted three riders galloping toward him from Grandee. One of them he recognized as Miguel. The others must be vaqueros who had come in after he had left.

He waited until they reached him. Then he said, "All right, let's go. Miguel, you ride ahead until you spot them."

Miguel pounded away. Jason held his pace to a steady walk, resting the horses for the time when they would need all the strength they had. At least he wasn't outnumbered now. The vaquero had counted nine men in Sheets' camp yesterday. With the two Miguel had just brought from Grandee headquarters, Jason now had ten.

Weariness rolled over him in waves. He turned his head, saw the same weariness in the faces of his men. He glanced at the sky. In half an hour it would be dark.

Perhaps Sheets' group had waited for Juan, he realized suddenly. That explained why they had not already reached Grandee. They wanted the legality that Juan's presence with them would lend.

If they weren't located soon, it would mean they probably didn't intend to attack Grandee tonight. They'd wait for dawn. But Jason wouldn't wait that long. He'd hit them in the dark. In darkness it wouldn't be so readily apparent that Jason's men were tired. Besides, an illusion of greater numbers could be maintained.

The last thin rim of the sun sank from sight. High clouds were stained briefly by its dying rays. Then the sky turned gray and dusk settled softly across the land.

The horses plodded along patiently. In the last, gray light of dusk, Miguel materialized out of the gloom ahead and said excitedly, "Señor, they are camped in a little draw about two miles from here."

"Is Juan with them?"

"Si, señor."

Jason said, turning his head, "All right. Dismount. Take it easy until I get back." He added, "Come on, Miguel," and rode away, heading east.

He wanted to see their camp for himself, and to learn all he could about the land surrounding it. He'd have to have every natural advantage he could get.

They rode in silence for most of the distance. Then Miguel said, "We had better leave our horses now, señor."

Jason swung to the ground, tied his horse to a small clump of brush, and followed Miguel, limping painfully. At last Miguel stopped and put a hand on Jason's arm. He got down and began to crawl, and Jason followed suit. They traveled for a couple of hundred yards this way.

At last Miguel whispered, "There, señor."

There was no fire, and the camp was almost impossible to see. Jason had to fix his eyes on the spot for a long time before he was able to make out the shapes of horses and men. Some of the men were sitting, some moving around. The horses seemed to drowse.

Jason lifted his glances to the land beyond the camp. It rose from the campsite in a long, low rise for about a quarter mile. The land on this side rose well, to where Jason and Miguel lay. It was too open, he realized. There was no natural cover for a sudden attack. Those horses down there would give the alarm too soon.

He nodded and whispered, "All right, Miguel. Let's go back."

The two crawled carefully back from the crest of the ridge. They reached their horses, mounted, and returned along the way they had come. Jason frowned. One thing only could give him the advantage he had to have. They'd have to wait until very late, when the invaders were asleep. An attack then might have a chance to succeed.

Reaching the men, Jason said, "Take a couple of hours' rest. Sleep if you want. But no fires."

He dismounted and stretched out on the ground, the horse's reins looped around his wrist. He closed his eyes. His head whirled. His mind kept seeing Edie as she lay dying in his arms. Then Edie's face faded and he saw the arrogant, angry face of Juan Robles in the courtyard at Grandee.

Faces. His past was made up of faces, most of them dead. The irony of Sandoval Robles' offer struck him. A chance to change his life of killing, earned by more killing. He dozed fitfully, coming awake at short intervals to check the position of moon and stars. At last he got stiffly to his feet.

He called softly, "All right. It's time."

The men around him got up silently. They tightened cinches previously loosened, checked their weapons, and silently mounted. Jason and Miguel led out. When they reached the spot where he and Miguel had dismounted earlier, Jason halted them.

"Half of you go to the right with Miguel. I'll take the other half to the left. We'll hit 'em from both sides."

There was a soft murmur of assenting voices. Jason hesitated for a moment. He knew he should issue the order to exterminate the invaders. But when the words came they were, "Get their horses first if possible. If you can't, then get the men."

"Si. Si, señor."

Jason murmured, "Jethro, go with Miguel. Peligan, you come with me," and he wondered at himself afterward for saying it. Didn't he fully trust the pair?

It wasn't exactly lack of trust, he decided finally. It was that he knew the bond between men who earn their living by the gun. Jethro and Peligan might be reluctant, when the showdown came, to fire on Delehanty, Moore and Brown, with whom they had shared quarters at Grandee. He shook his head. What Jethro and Peligan did would depend, he supposed, on which side they thought was going to win.

In almost complete silence they traveled the short remaining distance and at last could look directly down into the invaders' camp. It was quiet down there. No movement was visible save for the slight fidgeting of the horses. But suddenly, like a knife cutting the silent air, a horse nickered.

Jason turned his head and yelled, "Let's go!"

He sank the spurs as he shouted the words. His horse

leaped ahead. Down the slight grade he thundered, seeing now the shapes of men and horses coming down the opposite slope.

Behind him, the vaqueros were shouting excitedly. Some of them began to fire aimlessly at the camp. Orange flashes blossomed in the camp itself.

The flashes came too fast, Jason thought fleetingly. The men hadn't been sleeping down there at all, or they wouldn't have reached their weapons this soon. They must have been alert, and each must have had the reins of his horse looped around his wrist, or else they could not have mounted as quickly as they did.

Before he was halfway to the camp, Jason realized they were not fighting a surprised stationary force. They were fighting men on horseback, fully dressed, armed, and awake.

Until now there had been no sound from Miguel's men. Suddenly a howl and a flurry of shots racketed from the opposite slope. This, and only this, brought confusion to the ranks of men in the draw. They had been alert, but not alert enough. They had seen only Jason's force, had not been aware of Miguel's until now.

They milled, and were still milling when Jason charged into the middle of them. He fired pointblank at one rider and saw the man spill from the saddle. He fired again, hitting a horse in the neck. The horse somersaulted with a shrill nicker that was almost a screech. The rider, thrown clear, got up and began to run. He ran directly into Miguel's men and was literally riddled by half a dozen guns.

Then Jason and the men with him were through the

camp, and milling around with Miguel's riders on the other side. Jason heard Sheets' hoarse voice rallying his group, and saw them bunch.

The odds were better now, he thought. If Sheets elected to run, Jason's men would pursue and cut them down one by one. But Sheets' men did not run. Grouped, they suddenly charged directly at Jason's riders.

There was no yelling now. This was a fierce melee where it was difficult to tell friend from foe. Jason's horse was struck broadside and knocked to his knees. Jason spilled from the saddle. He struck on his wounded leg, but he did not lose his grip on his gun. Waves of dizziness rolled through his brain. He tasted grit in his mouth.

Somewhere a man was moaning. A little farther away a wounded horse was thrashing frantically. The battle moved slightly to one side. Jason pulled himself to his feet. He thought he heard the diminishing thunder of hoofs, but he could not be sure. He stared in all directions but saw nothing.

He stumbled to his horse, mounted painfully, and reined toward the still milling, battling group. A part of them suddenly split away from the others. They fled frantically across the plain. Thundering in pursuit, Jason counted them. There were only three.

He hauled his horse to a sudden halt, letting the others stream past and continue the pursuit. Frowning, he returned to the site of the camp. Five men were down on the ground. Three of these were motionless and probably dead. The other two. . . .

Jason went to them. One was Peligan. The other was

a vaquero named Felipe. He said, "We'll have a fire in a minute. Hold on."

He crossed to the first of the motionless ones. It was Brown, and he was dead. The second was a man Jason didn't know, also dead. The third was Dehehanty, breathing but obviously close to death.

And Jason remembered the sound of retreating hoofbeats he'd thought he'd heard as he regained full consciousness after that spill he'd had. He cursed softly, savagely, under his breath. Because he understood. Juan Robles, Sheets and Nordyke had deserted their men.

It had to be. Three of the group were here, dead or dying on the ground. Another three had fled, with Miguel and the vaqueros in pursuit. That left three unaccounted for. Where had they gone? Jason knew the answer to that before his mind had finished phrasing the question. They had gone to Grandee.

Cold terror gripped his mind. Clare was at Grandee. Clare was heir to half of it. But if Clare were to die, then it would all belong to Juan. He stared helplessly in the direction his men had gone. Why hadn't he stopped them? Why hadn't he guessed in time?

But he hadn't. And now it was too late. By the time he could reassemble his men and ride to Grandee, Juan, Sheets, and Nordyke would be in possession there. Clare would probably be dead.

Swiftly he gathered great armloads of dry grass, piled them near the wounded men, stripped a couple of saddles from horses that were down and put them on top of the pile. He struck a match.

In the increasing glow from the fire he examined

first Peligan's wound and then Felipe's. He laid a compress on Peligan's and told him to hold it there. He stared at Felipe's helplessly, knowing there was nothing he could do.

Then he hurried to his horse, mounted and spurred away in the direction of Grandee. He was already too late to save Grandee, but purhaps he would not be too late to save Clare's life.

Chapter 17

Under the merciless raking of his spurs, Jason's horse faltered, stumbled and almost fell. He allowed the animal to slow to a walk, seething inwardly at the loss of time. Time was his most important consideration right now. If he lost too much of it. . . .

When the horse was again breathing normally, Jason urged him to a trot. But the miles passed with agonizing slowness. And no plan formed in his mind. There was no plan which would give a lone man advantage over three. Three who were in possession of the house at Grandee. Three who would fire from ambush at a man necessarily exposed.

Behind Jason, the horizon showed a thin line of gray. In half an hour it would be light enough to see, light enough for the three at Grandee to shoot at him as he approached. He spurred the horse recklessly. If he killed the animal, it would have to be. He could afford no further loss of time.

The gray in the east grew stronger, but it had scarcely begun to spread across the sky when Grandee came into sight. He halted, concealed behind a low ridge, and scanned the place swiftly. Then he reined hard left and rode behind the ridge for half a mile before he turned and crossed it to drop into the bed of Caballo Creek.

Here there were a few scattered trees, thick brush half as high as a man on horseback, and an occasional cut which hid both him and his horse completely from sight. Between the last of the brush and the nearest adobe hut on the same side of the creek as the horse was an open space of about a hundred yards. Jason dismounted and tied his horse. Afoot, rifle in hand, he crouched and sprinted across the open space.

He was halfway across before a rifle roared from an upstairs window of the house. Dust geysered half a dozen feet to his right and just ahead of him. He flung himself to the ground, rolling, as the next shot racketed. The marksman had corrected his range, and this shot was closer. But because Jason was on the ground, it missed.

He scrambled frantically for the shelter of the adobe hut, and reached it, aware that exertion had reopened his leg wound. It was bleeding profusely.

He cursed softly and stood erect behind the hut, letting his breathing quiet and grow normal again. The whole sky was gray now and there was a golden cast to that part of it which was immediately above the eastern horizon. Ten more minutes and the sun would begin to rise. But he was here, and he was still alive. For now that was all that mattered to him.

There was an empty barrel behind the hut. He laid it on its side, kicked it and sent it rolling out into the narrow, dusty street between the rows of adobe huts. Immediately two rifles opened up from the house, riddling the barrel in seconds. But Jason had sprinted the other way as soon as the first shot sounded.

He reached a third row of huts. This one, angling slightly, afforded protection from the rifles if he stayed close to the walls. He moved along cautiously.

A dog crossed toward him, scampering and wagging its tail. Instantly the rifles opened up and the dog fell, writhing in the dust. Anger at the senselessness of it touched Jason, until he realized it had not been intentional. The pair with rifles up there were simply trigger happy. They were shooting at everything that moved.

He smiled grimly. Trigger-happy men were nervous men, fearful men. An encouraging development, until he thought of the added danger to Clare. He reached the wall surrounding the courtyard, breathing hard. The pain in his leg was increasing rapidly. So was the numbness in his foot and lower leg.

He had to get into the courtyard before he could enter the house. And there were only two ways of doing that—he could go over the wall, or he could go through the gate. Either course was impossible. The two in the upstairs windows of the house were shooting better than they had at first. Both the barrel and dog had been riddled almost instantly.

Where was the third man? he wondered. Probably waiting in the courtyard, covering the gate.

This place had been built, he realized, like a fortress to repel Indian attacks. The walls were too high to be scaled except with a ladder. And where there was no wall, the adobe walls of the house had no windows lower than twenty feet from the ground. He began to ease along the wall toward the gate. If he had to go in that way, he'd go in that way. There was no other alternative.

He heard a hoarse whisper, "Señor. Señor."

He turned his head. A woman was beckoning to him from behind one of the adobe shacks, one which was close enough to the wall to be concealed from the windows of the house.

He crossed to her warily. She was small, bowlegged and very old. She beckoned with a bony finger and he followed her into the hut.

The floor was of hard-packed earth. She pointed to a section of it and spoke rapidly in Spanish. "A tunnel is there, an escape tunnel dug by Sandoval Robles in the early days when Indians often attacked this place. It has been covered over for years and I am, perhaps, the only one left who knows about it. You can enter the house through it, señor. It will bring you into the kitchen."

Jason stared at the women. If he were trapped in the tunnel. . . . But she met his glance steadily, unflinchingly. He said, "Gracias, old one. Is there a shovel?"

"Si, señor."

She disappeared out the door and returned a moment later carrying a rusty shovel. Jason began to dig. He dug for nearly a foot into the hard-packed ground. At last the shovel struck some planks. He uncovered them, sweating heavily from exertion, aware of the increasing, throbbing pain in his leg. He pried them off, one by one.

A dry, cool, musty smell emanated from the dark hole. He said, "A lantern or candle?"

She brought him the stub of a candle. He lighted it and lowered himself into the hole. He could hear her replacing the planks, and was showered with dry dirt that fell from them as she did.

The candle flickered slightly as he crawled along the tunnel. It could be caved in someplace between here and the house, he realized. The exit could be nailed or plastered shut. But, he supposed, anything was better than trying to enter the courtyard by the gate. That was certain death.

He crawled for an interminable time, not hurrying, for he knew time was working to his advantage now. His disappearance would make his adversaries even more nervous than they had been before. They might even begin believing they had shot him, and would organize a search.

He encountered a cave-in, but the dirt was dry and powdery and he was able to tunnel through. At last he reached a point from which the tunnel began to rise steadily. He crawled upward and eventually reached a sort of landing where he could stand upright. Facing him was a heavy plank door.

He fixed the candle in a hollowed out niche in the dirt wall and felt the door with his hands. He had to get through, but he also had to avoid noise. He had to get into the house without letting them know he had.

Gently, he moved the door back and forth, loosening it. At last it gave and swung into the tunnel toward him. A second door was now exposed, of thinner boards. But no matter how he tugged, it refused to give.

He worked at it steadily for more than fifteen minutes, without result. The candle flickered and went out. The air in here was gone, he realized. He had run completely out of time. The choice now was to return along the way he had come and try to force his way up through the planks and two feet of earth, which the old woman would have replaced by now, or force the door regardless of the noise it made.

He frowned in the darkness. Half measures weren't going to work. Once he started trying to force the door, he would have to succeed quickly or he'd be trapped in here. The men inside the house would open the door, enter the tunnel and either kill him or starve him out—if he didn't die of suffocation first.

He leaned his rifle against the dirt wall to one side of the door, and shoved his revolver more firmly down into its holster. Then, bracing his back against the dirt wall, he brought both legs and feet up convulsively and kicked with all his strength against the door.

They struck with a thunderous hollow crash. The door gave a couple of inches and, on the other side, iron pots and pans crashed and rolled across the kitchen floor with a continuous crashing sound.

Again Jason brought up his feet and kicked. Then, seizing the rifle, he hit the door with his shoulder, driving with his legs. He plunged on through, stumbled on the pots littering the floor, and sprawled headlong, His rifle slipped from his hand.

As he rolled helplessly, his glance took in the kitchen, the location of the door, the startled Elena and the terrified serving girl. Then he gained his feet and plunged toward the door. He raced through it, diving aside as a gun blasted nearly in his face.

Sheets stood at the other end of the hall, gun in hand. It blasted a second time as Jason's own gun came out and up. It blasted a third time as Jason shot.

The second bullet raked his shoulder like a red-hot iron. The third struck his holster, ripped it and left it dangling from his cartridge belt. But Jason's bullet struck its mark unerringly. Sheets was driven back by the force of the heavy slug. A small spot of blood appeared almost in the center of his left shirt pocket.

He sat down helplessly. His gun barrel struck the floor. He tried to raise it, and the effort made blood vessels stand out starkly on his forehead and in his neck. Beads of sweat showed on his upper lip.

He said viciously, "You son-of-a-bitch! You dirty son-of-a-bitch!"

Then his body sagged. His eyes, still open, glazed and turned opaque.

Jason ran along the hallway, passed him, and dived on through the door. He was in the dining room, dominated by a fantastically long and heavy oaken table and by an equally heavy cabinet at the far end. There must have been twenty heavy oak chairs in the room, standing against the wall and around the table. The walls were hung with tapestries. The room was empty. So was that part of the huge living room beyond that Jason could see.

Sheets was dead, but there was still Nordyke, hating as Jason had seldom been hated before. And there was Juan Robles, who knew that unless Jason was killed he would lose Grandee, and probably his life as well. Juan and Nordyke must have been the two with rifles in the upstairs windows of the house.

He heard a voice yelling down the wide, curved stairway, "Sheets! You get him? Where the hell did he come from, anyway?"

Jason didn't answer the call. He realized that he was the one with the advantage now. Nordyke had to come down those stairs. As far as Jason knew, there was no other way. He moved silently to a point from which he could see the head of the stairs.

Nordyke's voice repeated, "Sheets!"

There was a long silence after that. Jason smiled grimly to himself. It was taking Nordyke a while to admit to himself that Sheets was dead, that it was Jason Mellor waiting at the bottom of the stairs.

How did Nordyke feel, he wondered, having to face Jason Mellor alone? How did he feel, going up against his brother's killer without half a dozen blood-hungry men at his back?

The question was answered almost immediately. There was a touch of panic in Nordyke's voice as he called, "Robles! Juan! He's down here. Come on!"

A voice, that of Juan Robles, answered in Spanish, too softly for Jason to understand the words. But it must have been a refusal, for Nordyke's voice came again. "This is your battle just as much as it is mine."

Jason spoke at last. "Nordyke? You hunted me like a wolf when you had half a dozen men to help. Now let's see if you've got as much guts as your younger brother had."

Instantly there was a flurry of movement at the top of the stairs. Nordyke came plunging down, making no effort to keep his feet under him, deliberately rolling instead. A desperate gamble, Jason thought. Nordyke would be shaken and bruised when he reached the foot of the stairs. It would take him an instant to orient himself and line out his gun.

He could have riddled Nordyke as he came rolling down the stairs. He didn't fully understand why he did not. An instant later he wished he had. Nordyke seized the ornate railing, halfway down, came to a sitting position on one of the steps, and raised his gun.

Jason fired instantly. The two shots sounded almost like a single shot. Nordyke twitched with the bullet's impact, stared at Jason with startled, unbelieving surprise, then continued his roll down the stairs. He stopped at the bottom, spread-eagled and dead.

A feeling of nausea touched Jason. Would there ever be an end of this? Or must he go on until he died, killing, and collecting in his memory ever more dead faces to parade through his dreams at night?

He licked his lips and swallowed, trying to get rid of the bitter taste. He stared at the head of the stairs. One more. One more. If he lived through that one, then perhaps he could know some peace at last.

Chapter 18

Juan Robles was upstairs. Jason had heard Juan's muffled voice a moment before. But where was Clare?

He stared at the stairway. It was wide, and there was a narrow balcony landing at the top which ended, at right and left, in hallway. Juan could be in either direction, then. And Jason would be exposed the instant he reached the head of the stairs. He holstered the gun long enough to stoop and slip off his boots. Then, drawing it again, he started silently up the stairs.

A couple of steps short of the top he halted, quieted his breathing and listened intently. He heard nothing—no sound of breathing, no slight scuffing of feet. But still he didn't move. Sooner or later Juan would make some sound. Then Jason would know, at least, which direction to face as he hit the balcony landing a few feet above.

Minutes ticked by, seeming like hours, like eternity. Pain and stiffness and wearines made Jason feel lightheaded. At last it came—the slightest of scuffing noises on the left.

Instantly he moved, charging the few remaining feet to the top. He reached the landing and turned toward the left, half crouching, his gun ready in his hand.

A blur of movement there. A racketing, echoing shot, and the blinding, choking cloud of powder smoke. He fired instantly, feeling as he did the tug of Juan's bullet against his ragged, dangling shirt. He plunged ahead before the smoke from his own gun had cleared, following Juan as the man fled through a door immediately on his right.

He heard a low moan and saw Clare lying on the floor beneath the window. There was a bloody bruise on her forehead. The moan had come from her, and had signaled her returning consciousness.

What had happened was suddenly very plain to Jason, even as his glance raked the room. Juan had been at the window, shooting at him as he approached. Clare had interfered. Juan had hit her with his gun.

Rage burned in him as his eyes fixed themselves on Juan. Juan babbled hastily, "Don't shoot, Mellor! Damn you, I've got my gun trained on her. Even if you hit me I'll get the trigger pulled."

"Maybe. Maybe not." Jason knew very surely that he was not going to be bluffed. He wasn't going to back out the door, leaving Juan with Clare. She stood between Juan and his ambition to own Grandee. He would kill her anyway. Jason stared straight into Juan's black eyes. There was triumph in their depth, as well as arrogance and contempt.

A man had certain skills. Jason's skill was his uncanny ability to shoot exactly where he was looking. He lowered his glance, fixing it on Juan's right arm. If he missed, now when it was more important than it had ever been before. . . .

If he missed. . . . Even if he didn't he would empty the gun into Juan immediately following that first important shot.

Staring fixedly at Juan's right arm, he tightened his finger on the trigger. Juan screeched. "Mellor!" as though guessing what Jason meant to do.

The sound of Jason's gun in the small room was deafening. And following it, like an echo, Juan's gun roared too, triggered by the reflex action through his smashed right arm.

The room was filled then, roaring with sound as Jason's gun fired again, and again. Juan slammed against the wall, held there in an upright position by the impact of each successive slug. Only when his gun was empty did Jason look at Clare.

There was shock and terror in her eyes. But she was all right. Oh God, she was all right. . . .

Without looking at Juan again, Jason crossed to her and helped her to her feet, putting himself between her and Juan so that she wouldn't have to look at him. He helped her out the door.

Death had come to this place, as Sandoval Robles had feared it would, But it was over now. Not again would Grandee's neighbors risk Grandee's wrath.

From the courtyard, sounds lifted, the sounds of many voices, of men, women, and children too. Jason and Clare went down the stairs and out into the baking summer sun.

The somber, worried faces of the vaqueros and their families softened into smiles. Clare looked up at

Jason's face, then returned her gaze to those crowding the courtyard. She said simply, in Spanish, "Thank you. Thank you very, very much."

And now she turned to Jason again. The things she was feeling were plain in her face and eyes. So was the promise that was in her heart. But she was a woman and so all she said was, "Now come inside and let me take care of you."